Agatha Christie

Crooked House

Collins

Collins

HarperCollins Publishers
The News Building
1 London Bridge Street
London SE1 9GF

www.collinselt.com

This *Collins English Readers* edition first published by HarperCollins Publishers 2012. This second edition published 2017.

10 9 8 7 6 5 4 3 2 1

First published in Great Britain by Collins 1949

www.agathachristie.com

ISBN: 978-0-00-826235-8

A catalogue record for this book is available from the British Library.

Cover design © HarperCollins*Publishers* Ltd/Agatha Christie Ltd 2017

Typeset by Davidson Publishing Solutions, Glasgow

Printed and bound by CPI Group (UK) Ltd., Croydon, CR0 4YY

Contents

◆ Introduction ◆

About Collins English Readers

Collins English Readers have been created for readers worldwide whose first language is not English. The stories are carefully graded to ensure that you, the reader, will both enjoy and benefit from your reading experience.

Words which are above the required reading level are underlined the first time they appear in a story. All underlined words are defined in the **Glossary** at the back of the book. Books at levels 1 and 2 take their definitions from the *Collins COBUILD Essential English Dictionary*, and books at levels 3 and above from the *Collins COBUILD Advanced English Dictionary*. Where appropriate, definitions are simplified for level and context.

Alongside the glossary, a **Character list** is provided to help the reader identify who is who, and how they are connected to each other. **Cultural notes** explain historical, cultural and other references. **Maps and diagrams** are provided where appropriate. A **downloadable recording** is also available of the full story. To access the audio, go to www.collinselt.com/eltreadersaudio. The password is the second word on page 3 of this book.

To support both teachers and learners, additional materials are available online at www.collinselt.com/readers. These include a **Plot synopsis** and **classroom activities** (both for teachers), **Student activities**, a **level checker** and much more.

Leonides Family Tree

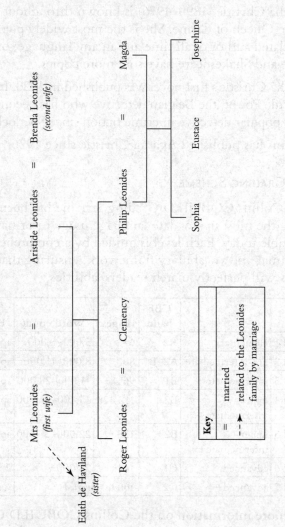

Key

=	married
- ->	related to the Leonides family by marriage

CHAPTER 1

There was a <u>crooked</u> man and he went a crooked mile.
He found a crooked <u>sixpence</u> beside a crooked <u>stile</u>.
He caught a crooked cat which caught a crooked mouse.
And they all lived together in a little crooked house.

—British <u>nursery rhyme</u>[1]

I first met Sophia Leonides in Egypt towards the end of World War II[2]. She had quite an important job working for the government, and when I worked with her I soon realized how good at her job she was, though she was only twenty-two.

As well as being very good-looking, Sophia had a clear mind and a delightful sense of humour. We became friends. She was easy to talk to and we enjoyed our dinners and dances together very much.

But it wasn't until I was ordered to go to East Asia at the end of the war in Europe that I realized I loved Sophia and wanted to marry her.

We were having dinner together when I realized this. It wasn't a surprise – I think I'd known for a long time that I loved her. I looked at Sophia and liked everything I saw. She had dark hair and bright blue eyes, a small chin and a straight nose. She looked very English.

Then suddenly I wondered if she really was as English as she looked – after all, her surname didn't sound English. Although we'd talked about many things, Sophia had never mentioned her home or her family. I didn't know anything about her background.

Sophia asked me what I was thinking about.

'You,' I replied truthfully. 'I may not see you for a few years, Sophia, but when I get back to England, I'm going to ask you to marry me.'

She sat there calmly.

'I'm not going to ask you now,' I continued, 'because you might say no and I'd be very unhappy. And if you say yes, I don't want to be engaged for years, or get married now and then leave you immediately. I want you to go home free and independent and decide what you really want. But I wanted to let you know how I – well – how I feel.'

'But you don't want to be too romantic?' murmured Sophia.

'Darling – don't you understand? I've tried not to say I love you –'

She stopped me. 'I *do* understand, Charles. And I like your funny way of doing things. You can come and see me when you get back – if you still want to—'

'Of course I'll want to,' I interrupted.

'You don't know that,' said Sophia. 'You don't know much about me, do you?'

'No,' I admitted. 'I don't even know where in England you live.'

'I live just outside London, at a place called Swinly Dean,' she said. '*In a little crooked house...*'

I must have looked surprised, because she explained why she had used the last line of a nursery rhyme. 'My family,' she said. '*And they all lived together in a little crooked house.* That's us. And though the house isn't really little, it's definitely crooked!'

'So do you have a large family?' I asked.

'One brother, one sister, a mother, a father, an uncle, an aunt by marriage, a grandfather, a <u>great-aunt</u> and a step-grandmother.'

'<u>My goodness</u>!' I <u>exclaimed</u> in surprise.

'Of course we don't normally all live together,' Sophia laughed. 'It was because of the war – with the bombing it was too dangerous to stay in London². But my grandfather takes care of us. He's over eighty and very small, but he's so alive that compared to him, everybody else seems rather boring.'

'He sounds interesting,' I said.

'He *is* interesting. He's from Greece, and his name is Aristide Leonides.' She added with a smile, 'And he's extremely rich. I wonder if you'll like him.'

'Do you?' I asked.

'More than anyone in the world,' said Sophia.

CHAPTER 2

More than two years passed before I returned to England. Sophia and I wrote to each other quite often. Our letters weren't love letters – they were about ideas and thoughts – but I knew my feelings for her were growing stronger and I believed she felt the same.

I returned to England on a soft grey day in September and immediately sent a <u>telegram</u> to Sophia[3].

> *Just arrived back. Will you have dinner this evening Mario's Restaurant nine o'clock. Charles.*

A couple of hours later I was at my father's house in London, reading the newspaper, when I saw the name 'Leonides' in the Deaths column[4].

LEONIDES – On September 19th at Three <u>Gables</u>, *Swinly Dean, Aristide Leonides, much loved husband of Brenda Leonides, passed away in his eighty-eighth year. Deeply missed.*

There was another announcement immediately below.

LEONIDES – Passed away suddenly, at his house, Three Gables, *Swinly Dean, Aristide Leonides. Deeply missed by his loving children and grandchildren.*

I thought it was strange that there were two announcements. There must have been a mistake. I quickly sent Sophia a second telegram.

> *Just seen news of your grandfather's death. Very sorry. Let me know when I can see you. Charles.*

A telegram from Sophia reached me at six o'clock.

Will be at Mario's nine o'clock. Sophia.

I was both nervous and excited at the thought of meeting Sophia again. I hadn't seen her for so long that when she walked through the door at Mario's it seemed completely <u>unreal</u>. We had drinks and then sat down to dinner. I said I was sorry about her grandfather, and we talked rather fast and were awkward with each other. It wasn't just because we hadn't seen each other for such a long time – I felt there was something definitely wrong with Sophia herself. Didn't she love me anymore? Had she met someone else?

Somehow I didn't think that was the problem. I didn't know what was wrong.

Then suddenly, as the waiter brought us our coffee, everything went back to normal. Sophia and I were together again, and it felt as if we had never been apart.

'*Sophia*,' I said.

'Charles!' she said immediately.

'Thank goodness that's over,' I said with relief. 'What was the matter with us?'

'It was probably my fault,' said Sophia. 'I was stupid. But it's all right now.'

We smiled at each other. 'Darling!' I said. 'How soon will you marry me?'

Her smile disappeared. The problem, whatever it was, was back.

'I don't know,' she said. 'I'm not sure, Charles, that I can ever marry you. Because – because of my grandfather's death.'

'Your grandfather's death? But what difference does that make?'

'Because I don't think he just died, Charles – I think he may have been – killed...'

I stared at her. 'But – what a very strange idea! Why do you think that?'

'It was the doctor – he wouldn't sign a <u>death certificate</u>, and the police need to investigate officially why he died. They clearly suspect that something is wrong.'

I didn't argue with her. Sophia was very intelligent, so I was sure she was right. 'But even if something *is* wrong,' I said, 'how does that affect you and me?'

'You work for the government – it might affect your job. No – please don't say anything – I know it doesn't matter to you. But it matters to *me*. I'm very proud – I want our marriage to be a good thing for both of us. And it *may* be all right – so long as the right person killed him.'

'What do you mean by "the right person", Sophia?'

'I know that's a horrible thing to say, but I'm trying to be honest.' Before I could speak, she continued, 'I'm not going to say any more, Charles. I've probably said too much already. But we can't make any plans until we know why my grandfather died.'

'At least tell me about it.'

She shook her head. 'No, Charles. I don't want to tell you what *I* think. Instead, I want you to see me – and my family – for yourself, from the outside.'

'And how will I do that?'

She looked at me with a strange light in her bright blue eyes. 'Your father will tell you,' she said.

I had told Sophia that my father was <u>Assistant Commissioner</u> of <u>Scotland Yard</u>[5], the London police headquarters. I suddenly felt cold. 'Is it such a serious <u>case</u>?' I asked.

'I think so. Do you see that man sitting by the door? He followed me from Swinly Dean. I shouldn't have left the house, but I wanted to see you, so I climbed out of the window.'

'Darling!'

'Well, never mind – we're here – together.' She paused and then added, 'And there's no doubt that we love each other.'

'No doubt at all,' I said. 'You and I have survived a world war, Sophia, so we can survive the sudden death of one old man. He probably just died of old age.'

'If you knew my grandfather,' said Sophia, 'you would be surprised that he died of *anything*!'

CHAPTER 3

I had always been interested in my father's police work – he was often in charge of important police investigations – but now that interest was personal.

My father had been out when I first arrived home, but this time when I returned from seeing Sophia, he was sitting at his desk. He jumped up when I came in. 'Charles! Well, well, it's been a long time.'

We hadn't seen each other for five years. Perhaps our first meeting after so long didn't seem very emotional, but my father and I are very fond of each other.

'I'm sorry I was out when you got here,' he said, 'but I've just got a new case.'

'Aristide Leonides?' I asked.

'How did you know that, Charles?' he asked with a <u>frown</u>.

'I met Sophia Leonides in Egypt,' I explained, 'and I'm going to marry her. She had dinner with me tonight – though she had to climb out of the window to meet me.'

My father smiled. 'She seems very independent,' he said. 'So you want to marry her? Well, it may be all right, if – if the right person killed him.'

That was the second time that night I'd heard those words. 'So who *is* the right person?'

He looked surprised. 'Didn't your girl tell you?'

'No. Sophia said she wanted me to see it all from the outside. I don't know anything about her family, except there are a lot of them.'

My father frowned and sat down. 'Very well, I'll tell you. Aristide Leonides left Greece and arrived in England when he was twenty-four.'

Just then the door opened and Chief Inspector Taverner came in. We'd known each other for many years, and said hello warmly.

'Taverner is in charge of the case,' explained my father, 'so he can correct me if I'm wrong. As I was saying, Leonides came to London and then started a restaurant, which was very successful. Soon he owned seven or eight restaurants, all making money, and then he started a large business – Associated Foods – supplying food all over the country.'

'Leonides had a natural ability for business and making money,' said Taverner, 'though of course he was always a bit dishonest – a bit <u>crooked</u>. He never actually broke the law, but he came close to doing so.'

'He doesn't sound a very attractive person,' I said.

'It's strange, but he *was* attractive,' said Taverner. 'He had a strong personality, and though he was short and rather ugly, women always fell in love with him.'

'He married a woman from a well-known family in the country,' said my father. 'Her parents didn't like it, but she was determined to marry him. And it was a very happy marriage, I believe. Leonides built a rather ridiculous-looking house at Swinly Dean and he and his wife lived there with their five children. Then his wife died.'

'Leaving him with five children?' I asked.

'Yes, but there are only two children still left alive,' said my father. 'Roger, the <u>eldest</u> son, who's married but has no children, and Philip, who married an actress and has three children – Sophia, Eustace and Josephine.'

'And now they all live together at the same house – *Three Gables*?' I said.

'That's right. Roger moved there after his house was bombed in the war, and Philip and his family have lived there for a few years. And there's an old aunt, Miss Edith de Haviland, sister of the first Mrs Leonides. She always hated Aristide Leonides, but when her sister died she came to look after the children.'

'Well, that's a big family,' I said. 'Who do you think killed Aristide Leonides?'

Taverner shook his head. 'I don't know,' he said. 'And we may never know. But he was certainly murdered – poisoned. There is one obvious <u>suspect</u>, but it will be very hard to get enough evidence.'

I looked at my father. 'In murder cases, Charles, it usually *is* the obvious suspect,' he said. 'Aristide Leonides married again, ten years ago, when he was seventy-seven. He married a young woman who worked in a tea shop.'

'And she's the obvious suspect?'

'Yes,' said Taverner. 'She's only thirty-four now and she's very close friends with a young man in the house who teaches the grandchildren.'

I looked at him thoughtfully. 'What was the poison?' I asked.

'The poison was called <u>eserine</u>,' replied Taverner. 'It was in the old man's <u>eyedrops</u>.'

'Leonides had <u>diabetes</u>,' added my father, 'and needed regular <u>injections</u> of <u>insulin</u>, which comes from the pharmacy in small bottles. Using a <u>syringe</u>, the needle is pushed into the top of the bottle and the insulin is taken up into the syringe for the injection.'[6]

I guessed the next bit. 'And it was eserine in the bottle, instead of insulin?'

'Exactly,' said Taverner.

'And who gave him the injection?' I asked.

'His wife.'

I understood now what Sophia meant by the 'right person'. 'Do the family like the second Mrs Leonides?' I asked.

'No,' replied Taverner. 'I don't think they speak much to each other.'

It all seemed very clear. 'So what's the problem?' I asked Taverner.

'If Mrs Leonides *did* do it, why didn't she change the bottle afterwards, so it was a real bottle of insulin? It would have been easy – there were plenty of bottles around. If she'd done that, I don't think that the doctor would have noticed anything wrong – not much is known about eserine poisoning. The doctor only realized it was eserine because he checked the bottle in case the insulin was the wrong strength.'

'So,' I said thoughtfully, 'Mrs Leonides was either very stupid – or very clever. Perhaps she hopes you'll think that nobody could be that stupid. Are there any other suspects?'

'Anyone in the house could have done it,' said my father quietly. 'There was plenty of insulin in the bathroom cupboard where anyone could take it. Someone could easily put eserine in one of the bottles, knowing it would be used at some time in the future.'

'Does anyone have a strong motive?'

My father sighed. 'Aristide Leonides was extremely rich,' he said, 'and though he gave his family plenty of money, perhaps one of them wanted more.'

'So you think it was his wife,' I said. 'Does her young man have any money?'

'Laurence Brown, the teacher? No, he's very poor.'

'What do you think of Mrs Leonides?' I asked Taverner.

'I don't know,' he replied slowly. 'She's very quiet – you don't know what she's thinking. And I imagine she likes an easy life – she reminds me of a big, lazy cat. But we need evidence.'

Yes, I thought. We all wanted evidence that Mrs Leonides had poisoned her husband – but no one was really sure that she had done it.

CHAPTER 4

The next day I went to the Leonides' family house – *Three Gables* – with Chief Inspector Taverner. I didn't really have any official connection to the case, but I had once worked with the police, and my father wanted to know all about the people in the house – from the inside.

'This is the kind of crime that may *never* be solved,' my father told me. 'Unless we can get some definite evidence, everyone in the family will always be under suspicion – including your Sophia. Why don't you ask her to help you?'

So here I was in Swinly Dean. Once we had driven past the golf course, we soon came to the front of the house.

It was incredible! The house should have been called *Eleven Gables*, not *Three Gables*. It looked like a traditional little country house, but one that was the size of a castle. It had lots of crooked gables and wood timbers – a little crooked house that had grown up suddenly, like a mushroom in the night! It was a Greek restaurant owner's idea of something English[7].

'It looks very strange, doesn't it?' said Taverner. 'It's actually one big house, divided into three separate houses – and all of them are very luxurious.'

Sophia came out of the front door, surprised – and not very pleased – to see me.

'Sophia, I've got to talk to you,' I said. 'Where can we go?'

For a moment I thought she was going to refuse, but then she led me across the grass and through a hedge to an untidy garden, where we sat down on a wooden seat.

'Well?' she said. She didn't sound very happy.

I told her what my father had said, and explained that the police needed definite evidence – otherwise the crime might never be solved. I asked if she would help me. Sophia listened very carefully. 'Your father is right,' she said. 'That's just what I've been thinking.'

After a pause, she said quietly, 'I *have* to know the truth! I have to know what happened to my grandfather.' She sounded almost desperate. 'I didn't tell you this last night, Charles, but I'm afraid.'

'Afraid?' I repeated.

'Yes – afraid,' said Sophia. 'Everybody thinks that it was Brenda – Grandfather's wife. I can say "Brenda probably did it", but *I don't really think she did*. I don't think she would take such a big risk.'

'What about the young teacher – Laurence Brown?'

'Laurence wouldn't have the courage,' said Sophia. 'Of course I could be wrong, but Brenda—' She shook her head. 'Brenda likes sitting around, eating sweets and having nice clothes and jewellery and reading cheap novels and going to the cinema. And I know he was eighty-seven, but my grandfather did make Brenda feel that she was an exciting and romantic person.'

But what Sophia had said earlier disturbed me. 'Why did you say that you were afraid?' I asked.

Sophia shivered. 'Because it's true,' she said in a quiet voice. 'I *am* afraid. We're a very strange family. We are all _ruthless_, in different ways. That's what's so disturbing.'

My face must have shown that I didn't understand, because Sophia continued, 'I'll try and explain. In Greece, Grandfather once stabbed two men in a fight. He told me about it in quite a relaxed way, as if it wasn't important. That's one kind of ruthlessness. And then there was my grandmother. I don't really remember her, but I've heard a lot about her. I think she was ruthless in a different way – she was always so sure that she knew the right thing to do, even in matters of life and death.'

'That sounds a bit unlikely,' I said doubtfully.

'Yes, perhaps, but I'm always rather afraid of people like that,' said Sophia. 'And then there's my own mother, who's an actress. She's a darling, but she only sees how things affect *her*. She doesn't think of anyone else. That's rather frightening, sometimes. And Clemency, Uncle Roger's wife – she's a scientist. She's ruthless too, in a cold way. She never shows her emotions. Uncle Roger's the exact opposite – he's the kindest and easiest person to love in the world, but he's got an extremely bad temper. Things make him so angry that he hardly knows what he's doing. And there's Father—'

Sophia paused. 'Father,' she said slowly, 'is almost *too* well controlled. You never know what he's thinking. He never shows any emotion at all. It worries me a little.'

'My dear Sophia,' I said, 'you're getting very worried about nothing. What you're really saying is that perhaps everybody is capable of murder.'

'I suppose that's true,' said Sophia. 'Even me.'

'Not you!'

'Oh yes, Charles, even me. I suppose I *could* murder someone… but only for something really important.'

I smiled, and so did Sophia.

'Perhaps I'm being stupid,' she said, 'but we have to find out the truth about Grandfather's death. We *have* to. If only it really *was* Brenda who killed him…'

Suddenly I felt rather sorry for Brenda Leonides.

CHAPTER 5

Just then we saw someone walking along the path towards us. 'Aunt Edith,' said Sophia, as we stood up. 'This is Charles Hayward. Charles, this is my great-aunt, Miss Edith de Haviland.'

Edith de Haviland was about seventy, with lots of untidy grey hair and sharp, intelligent-looking eyes. 'I've heard about you,' she said, shaking my hand. 'How is your father? I knew him when he was a boy.'

Rather surprised, I said he was very well.

'Have you come to help us?' asked Miss de Haviland. 'I do hope so. There are police all over the house.' She turned to Sophia. 'Nannie wants you, Sophia, about the fish for dinner.'

'Oh dear,' said Sophia. 'I'll go and sort it out.'

She walked quickly back towards the house, while Miss de Haviland and I followed her more slowly.

'I don't know what we'd do without Nannie,' remarked Miss de Haviland. 'She does so much work and has been here for so long.'

She stopped and pulled <u>viciously</u> at a big <u>weed</u> in the garden. 'I hate <u>bindweed</u>!' she said. 'It gets <u>tangled</u> up with the other plants and is impossible to get rid of.' She <u>ground</u> the weed viciously under her foot.

'This is a bad situation, Charles Hayward,' she continued, looking towards the house. 'I never liked Aristide Leonides – an ugly little man – but now he's dead the house seems so – empty. I've lived here over forty years, ever since my sister died and I came to look after the children.'

'And you've stayed here all that time?' I murmured.

'Yes,' she said. 'I could have left, I suppose, when the children grew up and married – but I loved the garden. And then when

Philip married and moved back here I helped look after *his* children.'

'What does Philip Leonides do?' I asked curiously.

'He writes books,' replied Miss de Haviland, 'history books. But nobody wants to read them. They don't earn him any money – but then he doesn't need to earn money. Aristide gave him over one hundred thousand pounds. And Roger is in charge of his biggest company, Associated Foods. All of them are financially independent. Sophia is regularly given a large amount of money to live on, and there's money saved in the bank for the other children.'

'So no one gains by his death?'

She looked at me strangely. 'Yes, they do,' she answered. 'They all get *more* money. But Aristide would have given it to them if they'd asked for it.'

'Do you have any idea who poisoned him, Miss de Haviland?'

'No, I don't,' she replied. 'It's upset me very much to think that we have a <u>poisoner</u> in the house. I suppose the police will think poor Brenda did it. She is rather stupid – perhaps she got tired of waiting for Aristide to die. If it *was* her, it will be all right – she isn't one of the family.'

'Do you have any other ideas?' I asked.

'What other ideas should I have?'

I wondered. She seemed to be intelligent. But as I looked at her I thought of the word Sophia had used – *ruthless*. I remembered how Miss de Haviland had viciously ground the bindweed under her foot. And just for a moment I wondered if Edith de Haviland had poisoned Aristide Leonides herself.

CHAPTER 6

We went back to the house and through the large hall. At the back, where there would normally be stairs, was a white wall with a door in it.

'You get to Aristide's part of the house through that door,' explained Miss de Haviland. 'Philip and Magda live in a different part of the house, here on the bottom floor.'

We went through a door on the left into a large <u>drawing</u> <u>room</u>. It had light blue walls, which were covered with many photographs and pictures of actors and dancers. There was a lot of heavy furniture and on the tables were large vases of flowers.

'Do you want to see Philip?' asked Miss de Haviland.

I had no idea, I thought – I'd only wanted to see Sophia. Should I talk to her father? If I did, should I say that I was a friend of Sophia's or that I was working with the police?

Miss de Haviland didn't give me time to say anything. 'We'll go to the library,' she decided, and led me out of the drawing room, along a corridor and through another door.

We entered a big, cold room full of books – not just on the bookshelves, but also on the chairs, tables and even the floor. A tall man of about fifty stood up as we came in. Philip Leonides was very handsome, which surprised me, since people said his father was so ugly. But this man had a perfect-looking face, with a straight nose and fair hair that was just beginning to turn grey.

'Philip,' said Edith de Haviland, 'this is Charles Hayward.'

'How do you do?' said Philip Leonides, shaking my hand. I couldn't tell if he had ever heard of me – he certainly didn't seem very interested.

'Are the police still here?' asked Miss de Haviland.

'I believe Chief Inspector Taverner is coming to talk to me soon,' Philip replied. 'I don't know where he is now.'

Just then the door <u>burst open</u> and a woman came in. She had big blue eyes and lots of red hair, and was wearing a luxurious, pink <u>dressing-gown</u>. She was talking very quickly in a clear, attractive voice. Somehow it seemed that three women – not just one – had entered the room.

'Darling!' she said, 'I simply can't decide what to wear at the <u>inquest</u>[8] – something dark of course, though not black – perhaps dark purple. How calm you are, Philip! How can you be so calm? Don't you realize we can leave this awful house now, and be free! Of course we could never leave when your grandfather – the poor old darling – was alive. He really did love us, but if we'd left, that woman upstairs would have made sure she got the house, the money – everything! But now, now we can produce that new play – and this murder will give us lots of free publicity!'

So this was Magda Leonides, Sophia's mother. 'I'm looking forward to talking to the Inspector,' she continued. 'He'll want to know exactly how and when everything happened, and I'll tell him all the little things I noticed and wondered about at the time—'

'Mother,' said Sophia, coming through the open door, 'you mustn't tell the Inspector a lot of lies.'

'Sophia – darling...'

'And I know you're ready to give a most beautiful performance – just as if you were acting in a play. But you've got it all wrong.'

Magda looked puzzled. 'What do you mean?'

'You have to act it in a different way,' said Sophia. 'Don't say much at all. Keep quiet and don't talk much, as if you're protecting the family.'

A pleased little smile showed on Magda's face. 'Yes,' she said slowly. 'Yes. That's a good idea.'

'I've made you some breakfast,' added Sophia. 'It's in the drawing room.'

'Oh good – I'm hungry,' said Magda, and quickly left the room. Sophia started to follow her mother, then turned back to say, 'Chief Inspector Taverner is here to see you, Father. You don't mind if Charles stays, do you?'

I wasn't surprised when Philip Leonides looked confused, but all he said was, 'Oh, certainly – certainly,' in a rather uncertain voice.

Chief Inspector Taverner came in. He looked calm and business-like. As I sat down in the background, Miss de Haviland said, 'Do you want me to stay, Chief Inspector?'

'Not now, Miss de Haviland, but I do want to talk to you later.'

'Of course. I'll be upstairs.' She went out, shutting the door behind her.

'I won't disturb you for long,' said Taverner, 'but I can now confirm that your father did not die a natural death. He was poisoned by a drug called eserine.'

Philip did not show any emotion. 'He must have taken the poison by accident,' he said. 'My father was nearly ninety and he couldn't see very well.'

'So you think your father put the contents of his eyedrop bottle into an insulin bottle,' said Taverner. 'Does that seem likely?'

Philip did not reply. His face still showed no emotion.

'We have found the empty eyedrop bottle,' continued the Chief Inspector. 'There were no <u>fingerprints</u> on it, which is strange – your father's fingerprints, at least, should have been there. Now, Mr Leonides,' he continued, 'can you tell me what you were doing on the day of your father's death?'

'Certainly,' replied Philip. 'I was here, in this room, all day – except when I went to eat, of course.'

'Did you see your father at all?'

'I said good morning to him after breakfast.'

'Were you alone with him then?'

'My – er – stepmother, Brenda, was in the room.'

'Is your father's part of the house completely separate from yours?' continued Taverner.

'Yes. The only way to get to it is through the door in the hall.'

'Is that door usually locked?'

'No, never,' replied Philip.

'So anyone could go freely between the different parts of the house?'

'Yes, that's true.'

'How did you first hear of your father's death?' asked the Inspector.

'My brother Roger – he lives on the floor above – came rushing down to tell me that my father couldn't breathe and seemed very ill.'

'What did you do?'

'I telephoned the doctor, but he was out, so I left an urgent message. Then I went upstairs. My father was clearly very ill, and he died before the doctor came.' There was no emotion in Philip's voice. It was a simple statement of fact.

'Where was the rest of your family?'

'My wife Magda was in London, but came home soon afterwards. Sophia was also out, I believe, but my two younger children, Eustace and Josephine, were at home.'

'And I'm afraid I have to ask you,' said Taverner, 'how your father's death affects your financial position.'

'My father made us financially independent many years ago,' Philip replied. 'He gave my brother Roger his largest company – Associated Foods – and gave me about one hundred and fifty thousand pounds. My father didn't keep much money for himself, but now he has made even more money than he had before.' For the first time Philip smiled slightly.

'So you and your brother don't live in this house because of financial problems?' asked Taverner.

'Certainly not. It's just easier for both of us, and my father liked us to live here. I was very fond of my father,' added Philip. 'I came to *Three Gables* with my family in 1937 and my brother Roger came in 1943, when his house in London was bombed.'

'I see,' said Taverner. 'Now, Mr Leonides, can you tell me anything about your father's <u>will</u> and how he has left his money?'[9]

'My father was not a secretive man,' said Philip. 'He held a meeting with all his family – and his lawyer, Mr Gaitskill – to tell us about his will. My stepmother Brenda was left one hundred thousand pounds, and the rest of his property was divided into three parts – one for me, one for my brother Roger, and the other was kept in the bank for his three grandchildren. I mean my children, Sophia, Eustace and Josephine.'

'Did your father leave anything to the servants?'

'No,' answered Philip. 'instead, their pay increased each year they stayed in his service.'

'And so you yourself don't need any more money, Mr Leonides?'

'I have enough money, Chief Inspector,' said Philip coldly, 'and if I needed more, my father would have given it to me. I had no financial reason to want my father dead.'

'I'm sorry for asking,' said Taverner, 'but I need to know all the facts. And now I have to ask you some rather personal questions about the relationship between your father and his wife. Were they happy together?'

'Yes, as far as I know,' said Philip.

'Did you approve of your father's second marriage?'

'My approval was not asked,' Philip said, 'but I didn't think the marriage was unwise.'

'It must have been quite a shock to you,' said the Inspector. Philip did not reply.

'Did you get on well with Mrs Leonides?' Taverner continued.

'Yes,' answered Philip, 'though I don't see her very often.'

'What can you tell me about Mr Laurence Brown, your children's teacher?'

'Not very much,' Philip said. 'My father employed him. His references were good, and he is a good enough teacher.'

'He lives in your father's part of the house, not here?'

'There was more room there.'

'Have you ever noticed any signs of a close relationship between Laurence Brown and your stepmother?' was Taverner's final question.

'No, I have not,' Philip replied.

Chief Inspector Taverner got up. 'Thank you very much for your help, Mr Leonides.'

I followed him out of the room. 'My goodness, Charles,' said Taverner, as we stood in the corridor, 'he's a cold man!'

CHAPTER 7

'And now let's talk to his wife Magda, the actress,' said Taverner. 'The name she uses on stage is Magda West.'

'I've heard her name,' I said. 'Is she a good actress?'

'She has starred once or twice in the big London theatres,' said Taverner, 'but she's never become famous – perhaps because she doesn't need to earn her living. If she wants to play a certain part, she sometimes finances the whole play herself.'

Sophia came out of the drawing room. 'My mother is in here, Chief Inspector.'

I followed Taverner into the big drawing room. For a moment I didn't recognize the woman who sat on the sofa – she was so different from the emotional woman in the luxurious pink dressing-gown I had seen earlier. Magda's red hair was now arranged in an old-fashioned style on the top of her head, and she wore a neat grey coat and skirt and a pale shirt.

'Please sit down, Inspector,' she said in a calm, quiet voice. 'How can I help you?'

'Thank you,' said Taverner. 'Can I ask where you were at the time of your father-in-law's death?'

'I was driving home from London,' Magda said. 'I'd had lunch with a friend and then gone shopping. When I got here, everything was in confusion. My father-in-law had become ill and was – dead.' Her voice shook just a little.

'Were you fond of your father-in-law?' asked the Inspector.

'We were all fond of him,' replied Magda. 'He was very good to us.'

'Do you get on well with Mrs Leonides?'

'We don't see very much of Brenda. We don't have much in common.'

'Was Mrs Leonides happy with her husband?'

'Oh, I think so,' replied Magda quietly.

'She is very friendly with Laurence Brown, I believe?'

Magda's body became stiff and she looked sadly at Taverner. 'Brenda,' she said with <u>dignity</u>, 'is friendly to *everyone*.'

'Do you like Laurence Brown?'

'He's very quiet – you don't really notice he's there.'

Taverner tried to shock her. 'Do you think Brenda Leonides and Laurence Brown were having a love affair?'

Magda stood up theatrically, as if she was on stage in a play. 'I have no idea, Inspector,' she said, 'and that is not a question you should ask me – Brenda was my father-in-law's wife.'

I felt like clapping her performance.

Taverner also stood up. 'Thank you, Mrs Leonides,' he said.

I followed Taverner out of the door to the stairs. 'I'm just going up to see Roger, the elder brother,' he explained.

'Can you help me, Taverner?' I said. 'If anyone asks me what I'm doing here, what should I say?'

Taverner smiled. 'Has anyone asked you?'

'Well – no,' I admitted.

'If no one has asked you, then don't explain or say anything,' he said simply. 'Everyone is too worried to ask *you* questions. Hmm,' he continued, 'this door isn't locked – none of them are in this house. You realize, of course, that all my questions about who was in the house that day don't matter at all?'

'Then why ask?' I said.

'Because I want to hear them talk,' Taverner said. 'I might learn something. Everybody in the house had the means and the opportunity to kill the old man – what I want is a motive.' He knocked on the door at the top of the stairs.

It was opened by a big, tall man, with strong shoulders, dark hair, and an ugly but pleasant face. 'You must be Chief Inspector

Taverner,' he said. 'I'm Roger Leonides. Do come into the sitting room.' He led us into a completely white room, which was light and <u>airy</u> and had very little furniture. It was very different to Magda's crowded room downstairs.

'I'll go and get my wife, Clemency,' said Roger. 'Oh, you're here, darling. I must get some cigarettes, if you don't mind.' He bumped into a table and went <u>clumsily</u> out of the room.

I looked at Clemency Leonides. She was about fifty, with short grey hair that suited her intelligent and sensitive face. Her eyes were grey and she wore a simple, red wool dress that fitted her slim figure perfectly. She had a strong personality, and I understood at once why Sophia had said she was ruthless. The room was cold and I shivered a little.

'Please sit down, Chief Inspector,' said Clemency in a quiet voice. 'Is there any news?'

'Your father-in-law died of eserine poisoning,' replied Taverner. 'It was definitely murder.'

'This will upset my husband very much,' said Clemency. 'He's a very emotional person and he loved his father very much.'

'Did you get on well with your father-in-law, Mrs Leonides?'

'I got on quite well with him,' she said quietly, 'but I didn't like him very much. I didn't like the way he did business.'

'What about Brenda Leonides – do you think she was having a love affair with Laurence Brown?'

'I don't think so,' said Clemency, 'but I don't really know.' She didn't sound at all interested.

Roger Leonides came hurrying back. 'Well, Chief Inspector? Is there any news?'

'Your father died of eserine poisoning,' explained Taverner.

'My goodness!' exclaimed Roger. 'So that woman murdered him! She couldn't wait for him to die!'

'Why do you think that?' Taverner asked.

'Who else could it be?' said Roger, walking quickly up and down the room, pulling his hair. 'I've never trusted Brenda – never liked her! None of us did. Why did Father marry her? At his age? It was madness – *madness*! My father was an amazing man, Chief Inspector. He did everything for me, and I – I failed him.' He sat down heavily.

'Now, Roger, please don't get upset,' said his wife quietly. 'Chief Inspector Taverner wants our help.'

'I'd like to <u>strangle</u> that woman with my own hands,' said Roger angrily. 'Yes, I'd strangle her! If she were here…' He was shaking with anger.

'Roger!' said Clemency sharply.

'Sorry, dearest,' said Roger, calming down. 'I do apologize. I – please excuse me—' he said to us, and went out of the room again.

'He wouldn't really hurt anyone,' said Clemency with a slight smile.

Taverner politely began to ask his routine questions, which Clemency Leonides answered clearly. Roger had been in London on the day of his father's death, working at the head office of Associated Foods. He had returned in the afternoon and had spent some time with his father. She herself had been at work in London, and had returned to the house just before six o'clock.

'Did you see your father-in-law on the day of his death?' asked Taverner.

'No,' replied Clemency. 'I saw him the day before, after dinner, but not on the day he died. I did go to his part of the house to get something for Roger, but I didn't disturb the old man.'

'When did you hear that he was ill?'

'Brenda came rushing over, just after half past six.'

I knew that these questions weren't important, but they gave Inspector Taverner the chance to look closely at the woman who answered them. Then Taverner asked if he could look round their part of the house. Clemency was surprised, but showed us the plain simple rooms, which were all very tidy and neat. Then she opened another door, saying, 'Roger will be in here – it's his own special room.'

'Come in,' said Roger, as his wife left us. His room was very different to those in the rest of the house. It was a personal room, full of papers, photographs and big chairs – and although it was untidy, it was pleasant and comfortable.

'I'm sorry about my behaviour earlier,' said Roger. 'I get very emotional at times.' He looked round to make sure that Clemency was not with us. 'My wife has been wonderful,' he said. 'I admire her so much. She's had such a hard life – she looked after her first husband, who died – and I was so glad when she agreed to marry me so I could take care of her. I'm so lucky – I'd do anything for her.'

Again Taverner politely began to ask his questions. 'When did you first know that your father was ill?'

'Brenda rushed over to tell me. I'd left him only half an hour before, and he was all right then. I rushed over to see him – he couldn't breathe properly – and then I ran down to Philip, who phoned for the doctor. I – we couldn't do anything to help.'

When Taverner and I left Roger's part of the house, the Chief Inspector said, 'He's very different to his brother, isn't he?'

I agreed with him.

'And the women they've married are very different, too,' Taverner added.

Clemency and Magda were indeed very different. And yet I thought that both married couples seemed happy together.

'But I don't think Roger is a poisoner,' continued Taverner, 'though his wife might be. No, I think it's much more likely to be Brenda Leonides – though I don't know if we'll ever get any evidence.'

CHAPTER 8

Now we went to Aristide Leonides' part of the house, where a servant opened the door and led us into a big drawing room.

Although it was the same size as Philip and Magda's drawing room, this room looked very different. It had bright sofas and luxurious curtains, and on the wall was a painting of a little old man. He had sharp, but kind-looking dark eyes, and crooked shoulders. He looked powerful and full of life.

'That's Aristide Leonides,' said Taverner. 'He certainly had a strong personality.'

'Yes,' I agreed, looking at the painting and the little man's lively, dark eyes. Now I understood why Edith de Haviland thought that the house seemed empty without him.

'There's a painting of his first wife over there,' said Taverner.

I looked at the picture of a typical English country lady. Her face was handsome, but rather dull and <u>lifeless</u> – not like her husband's face.

Just then the door opened and Aristide Leonides' second wife came into the room.

Brenda Leonides was quite pretty. She had brown hair, and was wearing a black dress and lots of expensive jewellery. She moved easily and lazily, like a cat. I noticed that though she wore make-up, she had obviously been crying. I also noticed that she looked frightened.

'Good morning, Mrs Leonides,' said Taverner. 'I'm sorry to disturb you again. You do understand, don't you, that you can have your lawyer here if you want?'

I wondered if she understood what these words meant. Apparently not.

'I don't like Mr Gaitskill,' said Brenda Leonides, sitting down on the sofa. 'I don't want him here.'

'We'll start, then,' said Taverner.

'Have you found out anything?' she asked, her hands <u>twisting</u> nervously.

'Yes,' said Taverner. 'Your husband definitely died from eserine poisoning.'

'You mean those eyedrops killed him?'

'That's right. You injected Mr Leonides with eserine, not insulin.'

'But I didn't know that!' exclaimed Brenda. 'I didn't have anything to do with it.'

'Then somebody must have deliberately replaced the insulin with the eyedrops.'

'It must have been an accident – or one of the servants,' said Brenda.

'We've interviewed the servants,' said Taverner, 'and we don't suspect any of them. Have you any other ideas, Mrs Leonides?"

She stared at him. 'I've no idea at all,' she said.

'You said you were at the cinema that afternoon?'

'Yes – I came in at half past six. I – I – gave my husband his injection, as usual, and then he – he became ill. I was terrified – I rushed to find Roger – I've told you all this before.'

'I'm sorry, Mrs Leonides,' said Taverner. 'Now can I speak to Mr Brown?'

'To Laurence? Why? He doesn't know anything about it.'

'I still want to speak to him.'

She stared at the Chief Inspector suspiciously. 'Laurence is in the schoolroom, teaching Eustace.'

Taverner and I left the room and walked down the corridor to a large room overlooking the garden. Inside a young man with fair hair of about thirty was sitting at a table with a handsome dark-haired boy of sixteen.

They looked up as we came in. Sophia's brother Eustace looked at me, while Laurence Brown stared at Chief Inspector Taverner. 'Oh – er – good morning, Inspector,' he said, looking very frightened.

'Good morning.' Taverner was <u>abrupt</u>. 'Can I have a word with you?'

'Yes, of course,' said Laurence Brown.

Eustace stood up. 'Do you want me to go away?' he said. His voice was pleasant but slightly arrogant.

'We – we can continue your lesson later,' said his teacher, and Eustace walked <u>stiffly</u> out through the door and shut it behind him.

'Well, Mr Brown,' said Taverner. 'I can confirm that Mr Leonides died of eserine poisoning, which was injected instead of insulin.'

'I can't believe it – it's incredible.'

'Would you like your lawyer here?' asked Taverner.

'I don't have a lawyer,' said Laurence Brown, 'and I don't want one. I have nothing to hide – I'm innocent – innocent!'

'I have not suggested anything else.' Taverner paused. 'Mrs Leonides was a lot younger than her husband, wasn't she?'

'I – I suppose so – I mean, well, yes.'

'She must have felt lonely sometimes?'

Laurence Brown did not answer.

'She must have liked having a friend near her own age living here.'

'I – no, not at all – I mean – I don't know.'

'It would be natural that you two should have become more than friends.'

'We did not!' insisted the young man. 'I know what you're thinking, but you're wrong! Mrs Leonides was always very kind to me and I respect her – but nothing more! And I – I wouldn't kill *anybody* – I'm very sensitive, and I'm not very strong. I object to killing – I wouldn't fight in the war. They let me teach instead, and I've done my best here with Eustace, and Josephine – she's a very intelligent child, but difficult. Everybody has been very kind to me – and now this awful thing happens. And you suspect me – *me* – of murder!'

Chief Inspector Taverner looked at him closely. 'I haven't said that,' he remarked.

'But you think so! They all think so! They look at me. I – I can't go on talking to you. I'm not well.' He hurried out of the room.

'He's really scared,' said Taverner, 'but that doesn't prove anything. Is he a murderer?'

'I don't know if he'd have the courage,' I said.

'This murder didn't need courage,' said the Chief Inspector. 'All he had to do was switch two bottles. Then he could marry a very rich woman. It's a shame that the servants haven't seen anything going on between them.'

He sighed. 'But it's all theory,' he admitted. 'It's more likely to be the wife, Brenda... though why didn't she throw away the insulin bottle – or wash it?'

He looked at me. 'Go back and talk to her, Charles. I'd like to know what you think.'

CHAPTER 9

I found Brenda Leonides sitting exactly where we had left her. 'Is Inspector Taverner coming back?' she asked abruptly.

'Not now,' I replied.

'Who are you?'

At last someone had asked me that question. 'I'm with the police,' I said, 'but I'm also a friend of the family.'

'The family – I hate them all!' Brenda looked frightened and angry. 'They've always been horrible to me! Why shouldn't I marry their father? What did it matter to *them*? He'd already given them lots of money. And I was very fond of him.'

'I see,' I said.

'It's true,' Brenda said. 'I was sick of men. I wanted a home and someone to be nice to me. Aristide made me laugh – and he was clever. I'm sorry he's dead.'

She sat back on the sofa. 'I've been safe and happy here,' she said. 'Aristide gave me lovely things.' She looked at the expensive ring on her hand with a satisfied smile. 'And I was very nice to him. Do you know how we met?'

Brenda didn't wait for me to answer. 'I was working in a tea shop and brought him his lunch. I was crying and he asked me to sit down. I said I couldn't – I'd lose my job. "No, you won't," he said, "I own this place." He was a little old man but he had power. I told him what was wrong. I was a respectable girl but I was – I was in trouble. I was going to have a baby.'

She looked at me. 'Aristide was wonderful,' she said. 'We were married at once. Then I found out he was very rich – it was like a <u>fairy story</u>.'

Brenda smiled lazily, like a cat. 'And I'd made a mistake – I wasn't pregnant. I was a good wife to Aristide and made him happy. But his family — they were always there, living on his money. They were horrible to me. Roger hates me and Philip never speaks to me. And now they think I murdered their father, but I didn't — I *didn't*!'

I felt very sorry for her — she was alone and <u>helpless</u>, and all the Leonides family wanted to believe she was a murderer.

'And if they don't think that I did it, they think that Laurence did,' Brenda continued. 'He's so sensitive, and I've just tried to be kind to him. He has to teach those horrible children. Eustace is always rude to him — he's been ill, you know, and can't go back to school yet — but that's no reason to be rude. And Josephine — well, sometimes I think there's something wrong with Josephine. She likes to <u>sneak</u> and <u>spy on</u> people.'

I didn't really want to hear about the children just now.

'What chance do Laurence and I have against the rest of the family?' Brenda asked me. 'It could have been one of them who killed Aristide.'

'They don't seem to have a motive,' I said.

'But *I* don't have a motive,' Brenda said, 'and nor does Laurence.'

'They might think,' I said, embarrassed, 'that you and — er — Laurence — are in love with each other and want to get married.'

She sat up straight. 'That's a <u>wicked</u> thing to say! And it's not true! I've been nice to Laurence but we're just friends, that's all. You do believe me, don't you?'

I did believe her. I believed that she and Laurence were just friends — though of course it was possible that she was in love with him without knowing it.

I was thinking about all this when I went downstairs to find Sophia, who was helping Nannie with lunch. She led me into the empty drawing room. 'Well,' she said, 'what did you think of Brenda?'

'I felt sorry for her.'

Sophia looked amused. 'I see,' she said. 'Yes, Brenda does seem to get on well with men.'

I was annoyed. 'I can see her point of view, that's all,' I said. 'Has anyone in your family ever been nice to her?'

'No, we haven't been nice to her,' said Sophia. 'Why should we be? You've seen Brenda's point of view, now see things from my side. I don't like the kind of woman who pretends she's going to have a baby so she can marry a rich old man.'

'Was she pretending about the baby?' I asked.

'I don't know, but I think so,' said Sophia. 'But she didn't fool Grandfather – he knew what he was doing and he got what he wanted. From his point of view the marriage was a complete success.'

'Was employing Laurence Brown as a teacher a success too?' I asked <u>ironically</u>.

Sophia frowned. 'Perhaps Grandfather wanted to keep Brenda happy and amused, by giving her a mild romance in her life with someone harmless like Laurence. I'm sure he didn't think it would end in his own murder. And that,' added Sophia, speaking with certainty, 'is why I don't really believe that Brenda or Laurence did it – because Grandfather would have known.'

'That sounds very unlikely,' I said doubtfully.

'But you didn't know Grandfather,' she answered. 'Is Laurence very frightened?'

'Yes, he is,' I said. 'I don't understand how any woman could fall in love with a weak man like him.'

'Don't you, Charles? Actually Laurence is very attractive. And you seemed to like Brenda very much.'

'Don't be silly,' I said. 'She's not even pretty.'

'No, but she made you feel sorry for her,' said Sophia. 'Brenda's not very pretty, and she's not very clever, but she does make trouble. She's made trouble, already, between you and me.'

'Sophia!' I exclaimed as she moved towards the door.

'Forget it, Charles. I must go to the kitchen and help Nannie with lunch.'

I remembered something that had puzzled me. 'Sophia, why do you have to do that? Why don't you have more servants in a house this size?'

'Sometimes we do have more servants,' she replied, 'but then Mother upsets them and they leave. Apart from Nannie, we don't have any permanent servants at the moment. So I have to help as much as I can.'

Sophia went off to the kitchen and I sat down in one of the big chairs to think. Upstairs I had heard Brenda's side of the story, and now I had heard Sophia's side. I realized that it was quite natural for Sophia and her family to dislike Brenda so much.

But I saw something that they didn't see. They were rich and powerful, with a safe place in society. They didn't know what it was like to be poor and helpless. Brenda Leonides had wanted pretty things and a safe home – and in exchange she had made her old husband happy. I felt sorry for her. I could see both her side of the story and Sophia's side – but who was right?

I hadn't slept well the night before and had got up early that morning. Now, in the warm room and the comfortable chair, my body relaxed and my eyes closed – and I went to sleep.

CHAPTER 10

I woke up so slowly that at first I didn't realize that I'd been sleeping.

In front of me I saw a human face – a round face with a big forehead, combed back hair and small, black eyes. The face was attached to a small thin body, and was looking at me closely.

'Hello,' said the face. 'I'm Josephine.'

I had already guessed that this was Sophia's sister. Josephine was an ugly little girl, about eleven or twelve years old, who looked very like her grandfather.

'You're Sophia's young man,' said Josephine. 'But why did you come here with Chief Inspector Taverner?'

'He's my friend,' I told her.

'Is he? I don't like him. I won't tell him things.'

'What sort of things?'

'The things I know. I know a lot of things. I like knowing things.'

She sat down and continued to look at me closely. 'Grandfather's been murdered. Did you know?'

'Yes,' I said. 'I knew.'

'He was poisoned. With es-er-ine.' She said the word very carefully. 'It's interesting, isn't it?'

'I suppose it is.'

'Eustace and I are very interested. We like detective stories. I'm being a detective now. I'm collecting clues.'

She was rather a strange child, I thought.

'I think there'll be a lot of changes here now,' Josephine told me. 'We'll go and live in a house in London. Mother will be very pleased. Father couldn't afford it before. He lost lots of money on one of Mother's plays. Grandfather wouldn't pay for it. He said it would be a failure, but Mother didn't listen.'

'I'm sorry the play was a failure,' I said.

'Yes, Mother was very upset. The things they said in the newspapers were so bad that she cried all day and threw her breakfast at one of the servants, who left. It was rather fun.'

'Are you sorry your grandfather is dead?' I asked.

'Not really. I didn't like him much. He stopped me learning to be a ballet dancer.'

'Did you want to learn ballet dancing?'

'Yes, and Mother and Father didn't mind, but Grandfather said I'd be no good.'

She stood up and danced a few steps round the chair. 'I suppose the house will be sold now. Unless Brenda goes on living here. And I suppose Uncle Roger and Aunt Clemency won't be going away now.'

'Were they going away?' I asked curiously.

'Yes. They were going on Tuesday,' said Josephine. 'Abroad somewhere. It was a secret. They weren't going to tell anyone until after they'd gone. They were going to leave a note behind for Grandfather.'

'Josephine, do you know why your Uncle Roger was going away?' I said.

She looked at me slyly. 'It was something to do with Uncle Roger's office in London. I think – but I'm not sure – that he'd "embezzled" something. That means stealing money.'

'Why do you think that?'

Josephine came so near that I could feel her breath on my face. 'The day that Grandfather was poisoned, he and Uncle Roger were shut up in a room together for a long time. They were talking and talking. And Uncle Roger was very upset. He said he was a failure – and that he wasn't upset because of the money, but because Grandfather had trusted him.'

I looked at her. 'Josephine,' I said, 'did you listen at the door?'

Josephine nodded her head. 'Yes,' she said. 'You have to listen at doors if you want to find out things. I'm sure the police do – and they look in people's desks and read all their letters, and find out all their secrets. But they're stupid! They don't know where to look!'

Josephine spoke coldly, as if she was better than the police. I didn't really notice the importance of what she said.

The unpleasant child continued, 'Eustace and I know lots of things – but I know more than Eustace does. And I won't tell him. He says women can't be great detectives. But they can. I'm going to write down everything in a little black notebook and then, when the police are completely confused, I'll tell them who the murderer is.'

'Do you read a lot of detective stories, Josephine?'

'Yes, lots.'

'And do you know who killed your grandfather?'

'Well, I think so – but I need to find a few more clues.' She paused and added, 'Chief Inspector Taverner thinks that Brenda did it, doesn't he? Or Brenda and Laurence together because they're in love with each other.'

'You shouldn't say things like that, Josephine.'

'Why not? They *are* in love with each other.'

'You don't know that.'

'Yes, I do. They write to each other. Love letters.'

'Josephine! How do you know that?'

'Because I've read them. They're very <u>soppy</u> letters. But Laurence *is* soppy. He was too frightened to fight in the war.'

Just at that moment a car arrived outside, and Josephine ran to look out of the window. 'It's Mr Gaitskill, Grandfather's lawyer,' she said. 'I expect he's come about the will.' Very excited, she hurried from the room.

A few minutes later Sophia and her mother Magda entered with a small elderly man.

'Your husband asked me to bring his father's will,' the lawyer was saying to Magda, 'but I don't have it. Do you know anything about it?'

'About poor dear Grandfather's will?' Magda opened her eyes, astonished. 'No, of course not. He told us he'd sent it to you after he signed it.'

'But the police didn't find the will with Mr Leonides' private papers,' said Mr Gaitskill. 'I'll just go and talk to Chief Inspector Taverner.' He left the room.

'Darling,' said Magda to her daughter. 'I'm sure that wicked woman upstairs has destroyed it. I know I'm right.'

'Nonsense, Mother, she wouldn't do a stupid thing like that,' said Sophia.

'It wouldn't be stupid at all. If there's no will, she'll get everything.'

'Ssh – Mr Gaitskill's coming back.'

The lawyer re-entered the room with Philip Leonides and Chief Inspector Taverner. 'I've talked to the bank,' the Inspector was saying, 'but they don't have any private papers belonging to Mr Leonides.'

'I wonder if Roger or Aunt Edith knows anything,' said Philip. 'Sophia, can you ask them to come down here?'

But when the others arrived, they couldn't help.

'Father signed the will,' said Roger, 'and told us he was going to post it to Mr Gaitskill the next day.'

'I sent Mr Leonides his will ready for signing on November 24th,' Mr Gaitskill said. 'A week later he told me it had been signed and sent to his bank to keep it safe.'

'That's right,' said Roger eagerly. 'It was in November last year – you remember, Philip? – that Father read us the will.'

'And what did the will say?' asked Taverner.

'It was quite simple,' said Roger. 'Father left fifty thousand pounds to Aunt Edith and one hundred thousand pounds and this house to Brenda. The rest of Father's money and property was going to be divided into three parts, one for myself, one for Philip and the third for Sophia, Eustace and Josephine – and the money for the last two was going to be kept in the bank until Eustace and Josephine were twenty-one. I think that's right, isn't it, Mr Gaitskill?'

'That is correct,' agreed Mr Gaitskill, slightly annoyed that he hadn't been allowed to explain the will himself.

'Father read it out to us,' said Roger, 'and asked if we had any comments.'

'And Brenda said that she hated to hear her darling old Aristide talk about death,' added Magda quickly. 'And when he was dead, she didn't want any of his stupid money!'

'That's only what people of her class think they *ought* to say,' said Miss de Haviland coldly.

I realized suddenly how much Edith de Haviland disliked Brenda.

'And after reading the will, what happened next?' asked Inspector Taverner. 'Exactly how and when did Mr Leonides sign it?'

Roger looked round at his wife, so it was Clemency who answered the Inspector's question. 'My father-in-law put the will down on his desk and asked two of the servants to come in,' she said. 'He covered the will with a piece of paper so they couldn't read it, then signed the will and asked the servants to sign their own names under his signature.'

'That's right,' approved Mr Gaitskill. 'To be legal, a will must be signed in front of two <u>witnesses</u>, who must then sign at the same time[9].'

'And then what happened?' asked Taverner.

'My father-in-law thanked the servants and they went out,' said Clemency. 'Then he put the will in an envelope and said that he would send it to Mr Gaitskill the next day.'

'Do you all agree,' said Chief Inspector Taverner, looking round, 'that this is what happened?'

There were murmurs of agreement.

'You say that the will was on the desk,' continued Taverner. 'Were any of you near that desk?'

'No – we were sitting about five or six yards away,' said Clemency.

'And did Mr Leonides get up, or leave the desk, after reading the will and before signing it?'

'No.'

Chief Inspector Taverner took out an envelope and gave it to Mr Gaitskill. 'We found this with Mr Leonides' private papers,' he said to the lawyer. 'Please have a look and tell me what it is.'

Mr Gaitskill looked at the contents of the envelope with astonishment. 'I don't understand,' he said. 'This is the very same will – but it isn't signed!'

'Perhaps it's just a copy,' suggested Roger.

'No,' said the lawyer. 'No, it's the very same will that I prepared for Mr Leonides to sign – there is a small mark on the paper that I noticed at the time. I <u>swear</u> it's the exact same will.'

'But that's impossible!' exclaimed Philip, speaking with more excitement than I'd heard from him before. 'We saw both the servants and my father sign the will. Father couldn't see very well, but he was wearing his reading glasses that evening.'

'Yes, I remember that, too,' agreed Clemency.

'And nobody – you are all sure of that – went near the desk before the will was signed?' asked Taverner.

'Nobody went near the desk,' said Sophia. 'And Grandfather sat there all the time.'

'Then I don't see how the will was changed,' said Taverner.

'Perhaps the signatures were <u>erased</u> or rubbed out?' Roger suggested.

'But we would still be able to see signs of that,' said Mr Gaitskill. 'And there aren't any.'

The family looked at one another.

'We were all there,' said Roger. 'It just couldn't have happened.'

Miss de Haviland coughed. 'But it *did* happen,' she remarked. 'What I'd like to know is what happens next?'

'It is an interesting legal problem,' said Mr Gaitskill. 'This will, of course, cancels all previous wills, and a large number of witnesses saw Mr Leonides sign it.'

Taverner looked at his watch. 'I'm afraid,' he said, 'I must go now.'

Everybody stood up, and I went quietly towards Sophia and asked if I should go, too.

'Yes, I think that's best,' agreed Sophia. I followed Taverner out of the room, and saw Josephine outside in the corridor. She appeared to be amused about something.

'The police are very stupid,' she said.

I arrived at my father's office at Scotland Yard to find Chief Inspector Taverner talking about the case. 'I haven't discovered anything at all,' he was explaining sadly. 'I can't find a financial motive – they all have enough money – and there's no evidence that Brenda Leonides and Laurence Brown were having a love affair.'

'I can do better than that,' I said, sitting down. 'Roger Leonides and his wife Clemency were planning to go abroad. Roger and his father had an emotional interview on the day of the old man's death. Aristide Leonides had found out something was wrong, and Roger admitted it.'

'How do you know that?' demanded Taverner.

'A private detective told me.' I explained to them about Josephine and how she thought Roger had been stealing money from his company.

'It sounds as if the child knows everything that happens in that house,' my father commented.

'If this information is true, it changes everything!' said Taverner. 'If Roger was stealing money from the company and his father found out, then Roger had a motive for killing him. Brenda Leonides was out at the cinema. All Roger had to do was go to his father's bathroom, empty out an insulin bottle and fill it up with eserine. Or perhaps his wife Clemency did it. She admitted that she went over to Aristide Leonides' part of the house and I think she's quite capable of poisoning someone.'

'I still don't think that Roger would use poison to kill someone,' I said, 'but I agree that Clemency might.' I had liked Roger. 'I don't think that Clemency cares about money – but she does care about her husband. For him she could be – well, ruthless.'

◆ ◆ ◆

The next day Taverner and my father had news. 'Roger's company, Associated Foods, is definitely going to go <u>bankrupt</u>[10] soon,' reported Taverner, looking pleased and slightly excited. 'It's been badly managed for years.'

'By Roger Leonides?' I asked.

'Yes, he's in charge,' said Taverner. 'But we don't think he's been stealing money. He just doesn't know how to run a business properly and has made lots of bad decisions.'

'Roger was only in charge of such a big company because he was Aristide Leonides' son,' my father remarked.

'He's been stupid,' added Taverner, 'but he hasn't done anything against the law.'

'So why commit murder?' I asked.

'Associated Foods needs a lot of money quickly to stop it going bankrupt,' explained Taverner. 'Roger <u>inherits</u> a lot of money now his father is dead. Though he won't get the money in time, the banks will give him credit and the company can be saved.'

'Why didn't Roger just ask his father for help?' I asked.

'I think he did,' said Taverner, 'and Josephine <u>overheard</u>. But the old man refused to give Roger the money.'

I thought that Taverner was right. Aristide Leonides was a generous man but he didn't like to waste money – he had refused to give Magda the money to produce her play. I thought it was unlikely that he would give Roger enough money – probably hundreds of thousands of pounds – to save Associated Foods. The only way for Roger to avoid financial ruin was if his father died. It was a strong motive for murder.

'I've asked Roger Leonides to come here to my office,' my father said. 'He'll be here soon.'

Sure enough, Roger soon arrived, bumping into a chair as he entered the room. In fact he was so clumsy that I couldn't imagine him putting eserine into an insulin bottle – surely he would have dropped the poison or broken the bottle?

'You wanted to see me?' said Roger eagerly. 'Oh, hello, Charles. I didn't see you. Have you found something?'

My father spoke coldly and officially, telling Roger about his legal rights and asking him if he wanted a lawyer.

Roger looked confused. 'But why am I here?' he asked. 'I've told you everything I know.'

'You did not tell us about the conversation you had with your father on the afternoon of his death,' said Taverner, 'about Associated Foods.'

Roger sat down suddenly, holding his face in his hands. 'I didn't think anybody knew about that.'

'You need to tell us the truth,' said Taverner. 'Will Associated Foods go bankrupt?'

'Yes,' admitted Roger. 'The company can't be saved now. I wish my father had died without ever knowing about it. I feel so ashamed. My father trusted me with his biggest company and I failed him.'

'Why did you and your wife plan to go abroad without telling anybody?' asked my father.

'I didn't do anything against the law,' said Roger, 'but I didn't want to tell my father about it. He was so fond of me and would offer to help. But I'm no good at business or managing a company. I've been so unhappy – I just wanted to escape from it all. Clemency – she's a wonderful woman! – agreed to go away with me without telling anyone, so we could live somewhere simply and quietly.'

'I see,' said my father slowly. 'So why did you change your mind and ask your father for help?'

Roger stared at him. 'But I didn't!' he exclaimed. 'My father found out himself. When he asked me about it, I told him everything. The dear old man was so good and kind to me. He insisted on giving me the money to save Associated Foods and wrote to his bank straight away.'

'Your father agreed to help you?' asked Taverner, astonished.

'Yes. I've still got the letter,' said Roger. 'I forgot to post it – I was so shocked and confused after Father's death.' He looked in his pockets. 'Here,' he said, finding the letter. 'Read it yourselves if you don't believe me.'

My father and Taverner read the letter eagerly – I read it later. Roger had told the truth. Aristide Leonides had asked his bank to give Associated Foods enough money to save the company from bankruptcy.

'What did you do after your father wrote this letter?' asked Taverner.

'I rushed back to my own part of the house and told Clemency what had happened – and how wonderful my father had been! About half an hour later Brenda came rushing in saying that Father was ill – just as I told you before.'

'So you didn't visit your father's bathroom at any time?' my father asked.

'I don't think so. No – no, I'm sure I didn't. Why, you don't think that I –'

My father stood up and managed to interrupt. 'Thank you, Mr Leonides,' he said, shaking Roger's hand. 'You have been very helpful – though you should have told us all this before.'

When Roger had left, I looked at the letter. 'So Aristide Leonides *was* going to help Roger,' said my father. 'That means that Roger had no motive for murder. In fact...' he paused, 'if Aristide Leonides had lived a day longer, Roger and Associated Foods would have been all right. But because he died so soon the company will now go bankrupt.'

'Maybe someone wanted Roger to fail?' suggested Taverner.

'What about the old man's will?' my father asked. 'Who actually gets the money now?'

Taverner sighed. 'The lawyers can't tell us. There is an old will but it was cancelled when the new will was made. But if Aristide Leonides died without a legal will – then his wife Brenda Leonides gets everything. She's the most likely person to have <u>played tricks with</u> the will – though I still have no idea how.'

I didn't know either. We were looking at the problem from the wrong way round.

CHAPTER 12

Chief Inspector Taverner left, and my father and I were alone. After a short silence, I asked, 'Dad, what are murderers like?' Now that murder had come so close to me, I wanted to know more about his previous police experience.

My father looked at me thoughtfully. 'Some of them' – he smiled sadly – 'are very nice, ordinary people... just like Roger Leonides.'

I looked surprised. 'Oh yes,' he continued. 'Murderers can be ordinary people who want something so much that they kill for it. They don't think about what happens next. And some people, although they *know* that murder is wrong, don't *feel* that it's wrong. They think that it wasn't their fault or that their victim deserved it – and they're never really sorry for what they did.'

'Do you think,' I asked, 'that someone could kill old Leonides if they hated him – hated him for a long time?'

'It's possible, but unlikely,' my father replied, looking at me curiously. 'People are more likely to kill those they love than those they hate. Only people you love can make your life impossible. But this doesn't help you, does it?' he added. 'What you really want to know is how to recognize a murderer in a house full of people who seem pleasant and normal?'

'Yes, that's right,' I admitted.

My father paused to think. 'The one thing that all murderers have in common,' he said finally, 'is that they are all <u>vain</u>. They are frightened of being caught, but they still want to show off about how clever they are. And a murderer wants to talk.'

'To talk?'

'Yes, because they're very lonely,' explained my father. 'They can't tell anyone about what they did or how clever they are – and they will *never* be able to tell. So they like talking about the murder. I think, Charles, that you should go back to *Three Gables* and get everyone to talk to you. Everyone in the family – guilty or innocent – will talk to you, because they can say things to you that they can't say to each other. And if the murderer talks, he or she might make a mistake and say too much.'

I told him then what Sophia had said about how the family was ruthless, in different ways.

He was very interested. 'Yes,' he said. 'Most families have a weakness, and it sounds as if both the de Haviland family and the Leonides family have a different kind of weakness. But I wouldn't worry too much about that, Charles. The best thing to do is to go and talk to them all. Only the truth can help you – and your Sophia.'

As I went out of the room, he added, 'And look after the child – Josephine. We don't want anything to happen to her.'

I stared at him.

'Come on, Charles, think!' he said. 'There's a murderer in that house, and Josephine seems to know everything that happens there.'

'She certainly knew all about Roger,' I agreed, 'and her story about what she overheard seems to be correct.'

'Yes,' said my father. 'A child's evidence is usually very reliable, even if we can't often use it in court. But children like to show off. If you want Josephine to tell you anything else, don't ask her questions – instead pretend that you think she doesn't know anything. But take care of her,' he added. 'It's possible that she knows too much.'

CHAPTER 13

As I went back to the Crooked House (as I called it in my own mind) I felt slightly guilty. I hadn't told my father and Chief Inspector Taverner what Josephine had said about Brenda Leonides and Laurence Brown writing love letters to each other. I told myself that it probably wasn't true. But really I didn't want to find any evidence against Brenda. I felt sorry for her, surrounded by a family who disliked her so much. And if there *were* any love letters, Taverner would soon find them.

And perhaps Josephine was wrong – though when I remembered the intelligence in her small black eyes, I doubted it.

I had phoned Sophia earlier. 'Please come, Charles,' she had said. 'The police keep searching the house, and we're all very nervous. I'll go crazy if I can't talk to someone.'

There was no one in sight as I drove up to the front door, which was open. As I stood there, wondering whether to ring the bell or to walk in, I heard a noise behind me. I turned my head and saw Josephine standing by the hedge, eating a large apple and looking at me.

'Hello, Josephine,' I said. She didn't answer, and disappeared behind the hedge. When I followed, I found her sitting on a wooden seat, swinging her legs. She looked at me coldly and didn't speak.

'Why wouldn't you speak to me when I said hello?' I asked.

'I didn't want to,' said Josephine, still eating her apple.

'Why not?'

'You sneaked to the police about Uncle Roger,' she said.

'Oh!' I said. 'But it's all right, Josephine. The police know that Roger didn't steal any money or do anything wrong.'

Josephine looked at me as if I was stupid. 'I wasn't worrying about Uncle Roger,' she said. 'But surely you know that in detective stories you never tell the police until the end?'

'Oh, I see,' I said. 'I'm sorry, Josephine. I'm really very sorry.'

'So you should be,' she replied. 'I trusted you.'

I said I was sorry again, and Josephine seemed to forgive me. She continued eating her apple.

'But the police would have found out anyway,' I said.

'Because Uncle Roger will be bankrupt?' As usual Josephine knew what was going on. 'Father and Mother and Uncle Roger and Aunt Edith are going to talk about it tonight. Aunt Edith wants to give Uncle Roger all her money – though she hasn't got it yet – but Father won't.'

Again I was impressed by how much she knew. 'Josephine,' I said, 'you told me that you were almost sure who the murderer was?'

'Well?'

'Who is it?' I asked. 'I promise I won't tell Inspector Taverner.'

'I want a few more clues first,' said Josephine, throwing away what was left of her apple. 'And I wouldn't tell *you*, anyway.'

'Then will you tell me more about the letters?' I asked.

'What letters?'

'The letters you said Laurence Brown and Brenda wrote to each other.'

'I made that up,' said Josephine. 'I often make things up. It amuses me.'

I stared at her, and she stared back. Somewhere, not very far away, a <u>twig</u> <u>snapped</u> with a sudden noise.

Rather late, I remembered my father's advice. 'Oh well,' I said, 'it's only a game for you. You don't really know anything.'

Josephine looked at me angrily, but she kept her mouth <u>firmly</u> shut.

I got up. 'I must go and find Sophia now,' I said. 'Come along.'

'I'm staying here,' said Josephine.

'No, you're not,' I insisted, pulling her to her feet. 'You're coming in with me.'

Josephine seemed surprised but decided to come in with me – probably to see how the family behaved when I arrived. It wasn't until I walked through the front door that I realized why I hadn't wanted Josephine to stay outside.

It was because of the sudden snapping of a twig.

CHAPTER 14

I heard voices coming from the big drawing room, but I didn't go in. Instead I walked down the corridor towards the kitchen and pushed open the door. There I found Nannie, a large, cheerful old woman. I knew she had worked for the family for many years, looking after the children.

'It's Mr Charles, isn't it?' she said. 'Come in and have a cup of tea.'

I sat down in the big comfortable kitchen, and Nannie brought me a cup of tea and two sweet biscuits. I felt like a small child again – I felt that I was safe and that everything was all right because Nannie was there.

'Miss Sophia will be glad you're here,' said Nannie. 'She's been getting very excited.' At that moment the door opened with a rush and Sophia came in.

'Oh, Charles!' she said. 'Oh, Nannie, I'm so glad he's here.'

'I know you are, dear.' Nannie smiled to herself and went into the room next door and shut the door behind her.

I put my arms round Sophia. 'Dearest,' I said. 'You're shaking. What's the matter?'

'I'm frightened, Charles,' said Sophia. 'I'm *frightened*. Someone in this house – someone I see and speak to every day – is a murderer. If only I knew who it was...'

I didn't know what to say. I wished I could take her home with me, away from this house.

'And the worst thing is,' she whispered, 'is that we may *never* know.'

I knew she was right, and that we might never know who poisoned Aristide Leonides. And then I remembered something I'd wanted to ask her.

'Tell me, Sophia,' I said. 'How many people in this house knew about your grandfather's eserine eyedrops, and that they were poisonous if injected?'

'That doesn't help, Charles,' she said, 'because we all knew. We were all with Grandfather one day after lunch when Brenda put the eserine drops in each of his eyes. Josephine asked why it said *Not to be taken* on the bottle of eyedrops. And Grandfather smiled and said, "If Brenda made a mistake and injected me with eyedrops instead of insulin, I would probably stop breathing and die, because my heart isn't very strong." Josephine said, "Ooh". We were all listening – we all heard him say it.'

So Aristide Leonides had actually told the murderer exactly how to kill him! I took a deep breath. Sophia seemed to know what I was thinking, and said, 'Yes, it's rather horrible, isn't it?'

Just then Nannie came back into the kitchen. She must have overheard what we were saying. 'I think you should forget about such horrible things as murder,' she said. 'Leave it to the police. It's their business, not yours.'

'But Nannie, don't you realize that someone in this house is a murderer?' said Sophia.

'Nonsense,' replied Nannie. 'The front door is open all the time. Anyone could get in to this house.' She again went into the room next door.

'Come on, Charles,' said Sophia. 'Let's go to the drawing room. There's a family meeting about Roger's business affairs. If you're going to marry me, you need to see what my family is really like.'

In the drawing room all the family were there, except Brenda and Josephine. Philip's face looked cold and serious, while Roger's face was red and he looked annoyed. Clemency, who was looking at the paintings on the wall, looked calm and cool, and Edith was sitting up very straight, doing some <u>knitting</u>. Magda and Eustace, both so good-looking, sat together on the sofa. Eustace's handsome face was unhappy.

As Sophia and I came in, everyone stopped talking and looked at us. Philip frowned. 'Sophia, this is a private family meeting,' he said coldly.

I heard the click of Miss de Haviland's knitting needles. 'Charles and I hope to get married,' Sophia said in a clear and determined voice. 'I want him to be here.'

'And why not?' said Roger. 'Charles knows all about it already!'

'Do sit down,' Clemency said. I looked at her gratefully as I found myself a chair.

The family meeting continued. 'I think we should do what Aristide wanted,' said Miss de Haviland. 'Roger, when the will is sorted out you can have my money to help save the company.'

Roger pulled at his hair. 'No, Aunt Edith. No!' he exclaimed.

'I suppose,' said Philip, 'that I might be able to give you a little money.'

'That's not very fair to our children,' said Magda quickly.

'I'm not going to take *anyone's* money!' Roger said excitedly.

'Of course he's not!' agreed Clemency.

'Anyway,' Magda added, 'Roger will have his own money when the will is sorted out.'

'But surely he won't have the money in time to save the company?' said Eustace angrily.

'Eustace is right,' said Roger. 'Nothing can stop Associated Foods from going bankrupt. It's too late.' He sounded almost pleased. 'And what does the company matter compared to the fact that Father is dead?'

'We are only trying to help,' Philip said stiffly, his face turning slightly red.

'I know, Phil, I know,' said Roger. 'But there's nothing you can do. It was all my fault – I was in charge.'

'Yes,' Philip said slowly, looking at him. 'You were in charge.'

Edith de Haviland stood up. 'I think we've talked enough about this,' she said with such power in her voice that everyone went quiet. It seemed that the family meeting was over.

Magda and Eustace got up and left the room, while Roger put his hand on Philip's arm and said, 'Thanks, Phil, for trying to help.' The brothers went out together followed by Sophia, who said that she would get my room ready as I was staying the night.

Edith de Haviland put away her knitting. She looked towards me as if she was going to speak, but she changed her mind, sighed, and went out after the others. I was left alone with Clemency, who was looking out of the window, and went to stand beside her.

'I'm glad that's over,' she said. 'Magda arranged it all – just like a play. Act II – the family meeting. There was nothing really to discuss.'

She sounded pleased about it rather than sad. 'Don't you understand?' she asked. 'We're *free* – at last! Roger has been unhappy for years – he was never any good at business, and it broke his heart because he failed his father. Roger loved his father a great deal – they all did.'

Clemency turned to look at me. 'It's ridiculous to think that Roger would have killed his father, especially for money. Roger was actually glad when he knew the company would go bankrupt. He was looking forward to our new life.'

'Where were you going?' I asked.

'To Barbados,' she replied. 'A cousin of mine died recently and left me a small house and some land. We'll be very poor, but we'll be together, away from all Roger's family. And I don't mind not having much money – I don't like money. I was happy with my first husband when we were poor – and I didn't love him like I love Roger.' She closed her eyes and smiled to herself. I could tell how strong her feelings were.

And I was sure that Clemency meant what she said. She wasn't interested in money, or living in luxury.

'Are you still going to Barbados?' I asked.

'Oh, yes, as soon as the police will let us. When everything has been sorted out we can leave – I hope it doesn't take too long.'

'Clemency,' I said, 'do you have any idea who did this? Any idea at all?'

She gave me a strange look, and when she spoke her voice sounded stiff and awkward. 'I'm a scientist – I deal with facts, not guesses. All I can say is that Brenda and Laurence are the obvious suspects.'

'So you think they did it?'

Clemency shrugged her shoulders, and stood for a moment as if she was listening. Then she went out of the room, passing Edith de Haviland on the way.

Edith came straight over to me. 'I want to talk to you,' she said, 'about Philip. I hope you didn't get the wrong idea about him – Philip is rather difficult to understand. He may seem cold, but he isn't really.'

'I didn't really think –' I began.

She didn't let me speak. 'Philip is really a dear, when you understand him. You see, Aristide loved all his children very much, but Roger – the oldest – was his true favourite. And I think Philip felt it, and though he always hides his feelings, he suffered – as children do. He's always been jealous of Roger, even if he doesn't realize it himself.'

'So do you think that Philip is secretly pleased that Roger's company has failed?'

'Yes,' said Miss de Haviland. 'I do think that. And it upset me that Philip didn't want to help Roger immediately.'

'Why should he?' I said. 'Roger is a grown man, with no children to think about. If he was ill or very poor, his family would help – but I'm sure Roger would prefer to start a new life without their help.'

'Yes, I'm sure he would,' said Miss de Haviland, 'and so would Clemency.'

She looked at me. 'I realize that this is all very difficult for Sophia,' she continued. 'I'm sorry that she has so much to deal with when she is still so young. I love them all, you know – Roger and Philip, and now Sophia, Eustace and Josephine. I love all my sister's children and grandchildren.'

She paused for a few moments. 'Yes, I really love them. But not *too* much,' she added, before turning abruptly and going out of the room.

I had the feeling that her last remark was important – but I did not understand it.

CHAPTER 15

'Your room's ready,' said Sophia.

We stood together, looking out of the window at the grey and windy garden. It was getting dark outside, and as we watched, two people came through the hedge and walked back towards the house.

The first person was Brenda Leonides. She was wearing a grey fur coat and moved quickly and easily like a cat. As she passed the window, I saw that she was smiling.

A few minutes later we saw Laurence Brown walk through the hedge. It didn't look as if he and Brenda had been for a normal walk – there was something secretive in the way they returned to the house. I wondered if it was Brenda's or Laurence's foot that had snapped the twig.

That made me think of Josephine, and I asked Sophia where she was.

'She's probably with Eustace in the schoolroom.' Sophia replied. 'I'm worried about Eustace.'

'Why?'

She frowned. 'He's behaving so strangely lately, since he's been ill. I don't know what he's thinking. Sometimes he seems to hate us all.'

'He'll probably change as he gets older. It's just a temporary thing.'

'Yes, I suppose so,' said Sophia. 'But I do worry – perhaps because Mother and Father don't. I didn't notice until I came back from the war, but they are a strange couple. Father lives in the past, with his history books, and Mother makes everything into a scene from a play. She arranged that meeting tonight because she was bored and wanted a dramatic scene.'

'Forget about your family, Sophia,' I said firmly.

'I wish I could. I was happy in Cairo when I could forget about them.'

I remembered that Sophia had never mentioned her home or her family.

'Is that why you never talked about them?' I asked. 'Because you wanted to forget them?'

'I think so. We're all too fond of each other and we all live too closely together – all together in a little crooked house. We haven't grown up separately and become independent. We're all tangled together and have grown up crooked.'

I remembered Edith de Haviland grinding the weed under her foot, just as Sophia added, 'Like bindweed.'

And then suddenly Magda burst through the door and turned on the lights. 'What an incredible scene that was,' she said. 'Eustace was so annoyed, and I love it when Roger gets angry and pulls his hair. And Edith really meant it when she offered Roger her money – she'd do *anything* for this family.'

'It must have been hard for her after her sister died,' I remarked, 'especially because she disliked old Leonides so much.'

'Disliked him?' interrupted Magda. 'Who told you that? Nonsense. She was in love with him.'

'Mother!' said Sophia.

'But she herself told me,' I argued, 'that she always disliked him.'

'She probably did when she first came here,' said Magda. 'She was angry with her sister for marrying him. But she was definitely in love with him – I know I'm right! Edith didn't like it when he married Brenda. She didn't like it *at all*!'

'You and Father didn't like it either,' said Sophia.

'No, of course we didn't,' said Magda, 'but Edith hated it most – I've seen the way she *looks* at Brenda.' Then she added, on a completely different subject, 'I've decided to send Josephine to school in Switzerland. It's not good for her to be here at the moment. I'm going to arrange it tomorrow.'

'Grandfather didn't want Josephine to go to school,' said Sophia slowly.

'Darling old Grandfather liked us all to live together, but I think that Josephine should be with other children. Switzerland is such a healthy place – it will be good for her.'

Magda stood up, smiled and went towards the door. 'Children must come first,' she said as she went out. It was a lovely <u>exit line</u>.

Sophia sighed. 'Mother is annoying when she gets a sudden idea. Why should Josephine be sent away to Switzerland in such a hurry?'

'It might be good for Josephine to go to school,' I said.

'Grandfather didn't think so,' argued Sophia.

I was slightly irritated. 'Did such an old man really know what was best for Josephine?' I asked.

'He *did* know best,' insisted Sophia, 'though I admit that Josephine is rather difficult. She likes to sneak around and spy on people, but only because she's playing at being a detective.'

I thought about how Josephine seemed to know everything that happened in the house. Perhaps Magda had another reason for suddenly sending Josephine to school – Switzerland was a long way away.

CHAPTER 16

As I washed my face the next morning, I thought about what I'd learned. People had talked to me, just as my father said they would.

The only person who hadn't talked to me was Philip Leonides. I thought that was strange, especially as he knew I wanted to marry his daughter. Edith de Haviland had told me that Philip had been an unhappy child, jealous of his brother Roger. Could Philip have killed his father – not for money, but so that Roger would be blamed for it?

I looked at my face in the mirror. What was I trying to do – prove that Sophia's father was a murderer? That wasn't what Sophia wanted!

Or – was it? Did Sophia herself suspect her father, and was she bravely trying to find out the truth? What did Edith de Haviland mean when she said she loved the family, but not 'too much'? And why had Clemency looked at me so strangely, before she said that Brenda and Laurence were the obvious suspects?

Everyone in the family wanted Brenda and Laurence to be guilty, but they didn't really believe it.

Of course, Brenda and Laurence *could* really be guilty, I thought. Or it could be Laurence, and not Brenda – that would be better. But that was only what I *wanted* to be true – it wasn't necessarily the truth.

Still, I wanted to talk to Laurence Brown, so after breakfast I decided to visit him in the schoolroom. As I went into Brenda's part of the house, I noticed that none of the doors was locked, and there was no one to see me as I went into Aristide Leonides' bathroom.

In the bathroom I looked in the cupboard and found the bottles of insulin and syringes. Everything was clear, well arranged and easy to get to. It was impossible for the police to find out who put the eyedrops in the insulin bottle – anyone could have done it.

As I went through the house, I didn't see anyone else, though I heard Edith de Haviland talking on the telephone. When I got to the schoolroom, I stopped outside the door to listen – I was behaving just like Josephine, I thought. I was very surprised to hear Laurence Brown talking with amazing imagination and enthusiasm – he was an excellent teacher. And although I didn't hear Josephine say much, when Eustace spoke, he showed that he was both interested and intelligent.

After a while the lesson ended and Eustace and Josephine came out. They looked surprised to see me, but while Eustace waited politely, Josephine went past me, uninterested.

I told Eustace I just wanted to see the schoolroom, and he opened the door for me. Laurence Brown looked up and then quickly left the room.

'You frightened him,' said Eustace.

'Do you like him?' I asked.

'Oh, he's all right. He knows a lot and he's a good teacher – he makes you see things differently.'

We talked for a while about history and poetry. Eustace, though he seemed to be bad-tempered, was an interesting person to talk to. I soon realized that he was bad tempered because of his illness, which had been frightening and difficult for him. Before his illness he had been enjoying his life and his time at school.

'I wish I was well enough to go back to school,' he told me. 'I was going to be in the football team. I hate staying home and having lessons with Josephine – she's only twelve.'

I said that Josephine was quite an intelligent girl for her age.

'*I* don't think so,' said her brother arrogantly. 'She's pretending to be a detective at the moment, sneaking around and writing things down in a little black book. It's just silly. Mother is quite right to send her to school.'

'Won't you miss her?' I asked.

'Miss Josephine? Of course not,' said Eustace, 'she's only a kid. Really, all my family are impossible to live with! Mother's always making a big drama about nothing, and Father's shut away with his books.'

I remembered how sensitive and embarrassed about my family I had been when I was sixteen. 'What about your grandfather?' I said. 'Do you miss him?'

A curious expression showed on Eustace's face. 'All Grandfather thought about was how to make money,' he said. 'He was too old to enjoy his life properly – it was time for him to die. He—'

Eustace stopped as Laurence Brown came back into the schoolroom. 'Please be back here at eleven, Eustace,' said Laurence. 'We've wasted too much time in the last few days.'

'OK, sir.' Eustace went out, leaving me alone with his teacher.

Laurence Brown was looking at me nervously. 'How are the police getting on?' he asked. His nose twitched, reminding me of a mouse in a trap. 'Are they going to arrest anyone soon?'

'I don't know,' I replied.

Laurence became even more nervous. 'You don't know what it's like,' he said quickly. 'Not knowing what the police really want – they keep asking strange questions…'

I let him keep talking.

'What Chief Inspector Taverner suggested – about Brenda Leonides and me,' he continued. 'It's just not true! The family has never liked me.'

His hands began to shake. 'They are rich and powerful – and I'm only a teacher. I didn't fight in the war – I knew I couldn't kill anyone! Everyone's always laughed at me. I always do things wrong. Everyone's against me. Whoever killed Mr Leonides arranged it so that I would be suspected.'

'What about Brenda Leonides?' I asked.

Laurence's face went red, and he suddenly behaved less like a mouse and more like a man.

'Brenda Leonides is an angel,' he said firmly. 'She is sweet and kind and would never poison anyone. The police are ridiculous if they suspect her!'

He went over to a bookcase and began sorting the books. I didn't think he was going to say any more, so I left him alone.

As I was walking along the corridor, a door on my left opened and Josephine suddenly appeared in front of me. Her face and hands were very dirty, and there was a spider's web in her hair.

'Where have you been, Josephine?'

Through the half-open door I could see steps leading up to a small <u>attic</u>.

Josephine replied briefly, 'Up in the attic. <u>Detecting</u>.'

'What is there to detect up in the attic?' I asked curiously.

'I must wash,' was all Josephine said, before going towards the bathroom. At the door she turned back to me and said, 'I think it's time for the next murder, don't you?'

'What do you mean – the next murder?' I asked with surprise.

'Well, in books there's always a second murder about now. Someone who knows something is killed before they can tell anyone.'

'You read too many detective stories, Josephine,' I said. 'Real life isn't like that.'

The only answer I got was the sound of water from a tap, so I left Josephine to wash. As I went back to the other part of the house, Brenda came out through the drawing room door and put her hand on my arm.

'Well?' she asked, looking up at my face.

I shook my head. 'I don't have any news.'

'I'm so frightened,' she said. 'Charles, I'm so frightened.'

Her fear was very real – I could feel it. She was so alone. I wanted to help her, to make her feel safe, but there was nothing I could do or say. I suddenly felt that Sophia was watching me, and remembered her saying, 'Yes, Brenda does seem to get on well with men.'

'The inquest is tomorrow,' Brenda said. 'And I'm sure there'll be newspaper reporters there.'

'Just don't talk to them,' I said. 'Perhaps you *should* get a lawyer, Brenda, to look after your interests and advise you what to say and do. You see,' I added, 'you're very much alone.'

Her hand held my arm more closely. 'Yes,' she said. 'You *do* understand, Charles. And you have helped.'

I went downstairs feeling warm and satisfied. Then I saw Sophia standing by the front door. 'You've been a long time,' she said coldly. 'Your father telephoned. He wants you to go back to London.'

'Did he say why?'

Sophia shook her head. Her eyes were anxious.

'Don't worry, darling,' I said, putting my arm around her. 'I'll soon be back.'

Chapter 17

When I arrived at his office at Scotland Yard, I found my father talking to Chief Inspector Taverner and Mr Gaitskill the lawyer, who seemed a little upset.

'Oh, hello, Charles,' said my father as I came in. 'Something rather surprising has happened.'

'Surprising!' exclaimed Mr Gaitskill.

'This morning,' continued my father, 'Mr Gaitskill received a letter from someone called Mr Agrodopolous, who is an old friend of Aristide Leonides. In with the letter was Aristide Leonides' will. Mr Leonides had asked Mr Agrodopolous to send the will to Mr Gaitskill after his death.'

'I have been Mr Leonides' lawyer for over forty years,' said Mr Gaitskill. 'Why didn't he trust me?' He was obviously upset.

'When Mr Gaitskill opened the will,' my father added, 'he decided that we should see it at once.'

'It is not the same will that I prepared,' said Mr Gaitskill. 'Mr Leonides wrote it himself – which is not a professional thing to do.'

This was all very interesting, but I didn't understand why I was involved. 'Is the will different?' I asked. 'I mean, is the money left to someone else?'

My father was looking at me. Chief Inspector Taverner was very carefully *not* looking at me. I felt slightly uneasy.

I looked at Mr Gaitskill. 'Am I right,' he said, 'in saying that you are going to marry Miss Sophia Leonides?'

'I hope to marry her,' I said, 'but she doesn't want to become engaged at the moment.'

'In this will,' said Mr Gaitskill, 'Aristide Leonides leaves his wife one hundred thousand pounds, and everything else to his granddaughter, Sophia Leonides.'

I was shocked – I hadn't expected this! 'But why did he leave everything to Sophia?' I asked.

'Mr Leonides explained his reasons in this letter, which was with the will,' said my father, handing me the letter to read.

Dear Gaitskill,

I am sorry that I have behaved so secretly. Let me explain why. I have always believed that in a family there is one strong character who looks after everyone else. In my family I was that person, and I have been lucky enough to live a long time and take care of my children and grandchildren. But when I die, someone else must take care of the family.

After much thought I have decided that neither of my sons is the right person to do this. My much loved son Roger has no business sense, and has poor <u>judgement</u>. My son Philip is too unsure of himself and is hiding from life. Eustace, my grandson, is very young and I do not think that he has enough sense, nor can he control himself. Only my granddaughter Sophia has intelligence, good judgement and courage – and is fair and generous. I believe she is the best person to take care of the family, including my sister-in-law Edith de Haviland, to whom I am very grateful for her lifelong care of my children and grandchildren.

Now I must explain why I kept my decision secret from you. I thought it best not to tell the family I was leaving everything to Sophia. I asked you to prepare a will, which I read out to all my family. I put both the wills on my desk and covered them with a piece of paper. When the servants came in, I moved up the piece of paper and we all signed the will that I wrote myself – not the will that you prepared[9].

Please forgive me for not telling you about this – I am an old man and wanted to keep it secret. Thank you, my dear friend, for all the care you have taken while dealing with my affairs. Give Sophia my love and ask her to take care of my family.

Yours very sincerely,

Aristide Leonides

'Extraordinary,' I said, after reading the letter.

'Most extraordinary,' said Mr Gaitskill. 'I repeat, I do think my old friend Mr Leonides could have trusted me.' He stood up and left the room, his professional pride obviously hurt.

'Now it's been explained, it seems obvious,' said Taverner. 'Aristide Leonides was the only person who could have played tricks with that will. We were stupid not to think of it.'

I remembered Josephine saying how stupid the police were. But she hadn't been there when the will was made, and I didn't think she could guess what her grandfather had done. So why did she say the police were stupid? Was she just showing off?

Suddenly I realized how quiet the room was. I looked up to see that both my father and Taverner were watching me. 'Sophia knew nothing about this!' I said. 'Nothing at all. She'll be amazed.'

'Will she?' asked my father.

There was a pause, which was ended by the sudden loud ring of the telephone on the desk. My father answered. 'It's your young woman,' he told me. 'She wants to speak to you. It's urgent.'

I took it from him. 'Sophia?' I said. 'What's the matter?'

'Charles? Is that you?' said Sophia, sounding very upset. 'It's – Josephine! She's been hit on the head and has <u>concussion</u>. She – the doctor says she may not recover...'

'Josephine's been <u>knocked out</u>,' I told my father and Taverner.

My father frowned. 'I told you to look after that child,' he said sharply.

CHAPTER 18

Taverner and I were immediately driven to Swinly Dean in a fast police car. On the way I remembered how Josephine had talked about a 'second murder'. The poor child hadn't known that she was to be the second victim. Josephine must know something about the murder that we didn't.

I remembered the snap of the twig in the garden. I should have taken better care of Josephine. Had Magda realized that her daughter was in danger? Was that why she suddenly wanted Josephine to go away to school in Switzerland?

As we arrived, Sophia came out to meet us. Josephine, she said, was in the local hospital, and Dr Gray would telephone as soon as there was any news.

'How did it happen?' asked Taverner.

Sophia led us round to the back of the house and through a door to a small yard. In one corner was an old wash-house. 'Josephine likes to play here,' she explained. The wash-house was small and dark inside, and full of wooden boxes and old broken furniture. Just inside the door was a stone doorstop.

'It's the door stop from the front door,' Sophia explained. 'It must have been balanced on top of the door.'

'A booby trap,' said Taverner, reaching up a hand to touch the top of the low door. Then he looked at the door stop. 'Has anyone touched this?'

'No,' said Sophia. 'I told everyone not to.'

'You're quite right. Who found her?'

'I did. She didn't come in for dinner at one o'clock. Nannie said she had seen Josephine go outside about quarter of an hour before. I said I would go and get her,' replied Sophia.

'Who knew that Josephine liked to play here?' asked Taverner.

'Everyone in the house knew,' Sophia said. 'No one really comes out here except her.'

'And you can't see this little yard from the house,' said Taverner thoughtfully. 'Anyone could have set that booby trap. He looked up at the door. 'She was unlucky,' he said. 'It could easily have missed her.' Next Taverner looked at the floor. There were various deep marks in it. 'It looks as if someone tried the doorstop out first, to see just where it would fall.'

'We didn't hear anything,' said Sophia. 'We had no idea until I found her lying face down.' Her voice shook. 'There was blood on her hair.'

'Is that Josephine's?' Taverner pointed to a wool scarf lying on the floor.

'Yes.'

Using the scarf, Taverner carefully picked up the stone doorstop. 'There may be fingerprints,' he explained, though he spoke without much hope. 'What are you looking at, Charles?'

I was examining an old wooden chair with a broken back, which was with the other old furniture. On the seat of the chair were a few small pieces of mud.

'Interesting,' said Taverner. 'Someone stood on that chair with muddy feet. Now why was that?'

I had no suggestions. Taverner shook his head. 'What time did you find Josephine, Miss Leonides?'

'About five minutes past one.'

'And Nannie saw her going out about twenty minutes earlier. Has anyone else been out here today?'

'I've no idea,' said Sophia. 'But Josephine herself was here after breakfast this morning.'

'So someone set the trap between then and a quarter to one. Did you notice that the doorstop was missing?'

Sophia shook her head. 'It's been too cold to have the door open today,' she explained.

'And do you know where everyone was this morning?'

'I went out for a walk,' replied Sophia. 'Eustace and Josephine had lessons until half past twelve – with a break at half past ten. I think Father has been in the library all morning, and Mother was just getting up when I came in at about a quarter past twelve. She doesn't get up very early.'

We went back into the house, and I followed Sophia to the library. Philip and Magda were sitting close together. Philip's face was white and Magda was crying.

'Have they telephoned from the hospital yet?' Sophia asked. Philip shook his head.

'Why wouldn't they let me go with her?' cried Magda. 'My baby – my funny, ugly baby. She hated it when I called her that. She'll die – I know she'll die.'

'Hush, my dear,' said Philip. 'Hush.'

I felt that I had no place in this sad family scene, so instead I went to find Nannie. She was sitting in the kitchen, crying quietly. 'This is all because of me, Mr Charles, because of the awful things I've been thinking.'

I didn't understand what she meant.

'There's wickedness in this house,' Nannie continued. 'I didn't want to see it or believe it. But somebody killed Mr Leonides and the same somebody has tried to kill Josephine.'

'But why should anyone try to kill Josephine?' I asked.

'You know what she's like, Mr Charles,' Nannie said. 'She always wants to know things and find out things. You see, she was always a very ordinary little girl, not good-looking like her brother and sister. Her mother sometimes ignored her and said she was ugly. Josephine hated that and it had a bad effect on her.

She started sneaking around and spying on people. But that isn't safe when there's a poisoner about!'

I murmured in agreement. And then I remembered something. 'Do you know where Josephine kept her little black book, where she wrote things down?' I asked Nannie.

'I've no idea, Mr Charles. It wasn't with her when she was found.'

Had someone taken Josephine's notebook? Or had she hidden it in her own room? I thought I would go and look. I went upstairs and stopped – I didn't know where Josephine's room was – but then I heard Taverner calling me:

'Come in here,' he said. 'I'm in the girl's room – it's a real mess.'

The small room was indeed a mess. Drawers had been pulled out and their contents thrown on the floor. Everything had been pulled off the small bed. The chairs had been turned over and the pictures taken down from the wall. Someone had been looking for something.

'Did anyone hear or see anything?' I asked.

'It seems not,' said Taverner. 'I've checked and anyone in the house could have done this – and set the booby trap. It could have been Philip, Magda, Nannie or your girl, Sophia. Brenda was alone all morning, Laurence Brown and Eustace had a half-hour break from lessons and Miss de Haviland was in the garden alone. Roger was in his study and even Clemency didn't go to work today. I've no idea who it was – or what they were looking for.'

I suddenly remembered where I had seen Josephine last. 'Wait!' I said, and ran out of the room and up the stairs to the attic, where Josephine had been 'detecting'. It was dark and the ceilings were low, but it was a good place to hide things, I thought, as I started to search properly. Indeed, it didn't take me long to find a packet of letters wrapped in brown paper.

I read the first letter.

Oh Laurence – my darling, my dear love… I'm sure everything will be all right. Aristide has been so good to me. I don't want him to suffer, but there can't be any pleasure in living when you're over eighty. Soon we shall be together for always. How wonderful it will be when I can call you my dear, dear husband. I love you, love you, love you…

I <u>grimly</u> went downstairs and gave Taverner the letters. 'This might be what someone was looking for,' I told him.

Taverner looked through the letters and read a few lines. Then he looked up at me, with a satisfied expression on his face.

'So it *was* them,' he said quietly. 'Brenda Leonides and Laurence Brown – it was them the whole time.'

CHAPTER 19

From the moment I found the letters all the sympathy and pity I had felt for Brenda Leonides disappeared completely. She had lied to me, and had tried to kill Josephine.

'But I think it was Laurence Brown who set that booby trap,' said Taverner. 'That explains what puzzled me about it. Josephine had the letters but the murderer couldn't find them, so he tried to kill her. But why didn't he just hit Josephine on the head himself? Putting a stone doorstop on top of a door is stupid. It could have missed or not hurt Josephine at all. So why do it?'

'Well,' I said, 'what's the answer?'

'At first I thought it was to fit in with someone's <u>alibi</u> – but no one *has* an alibi. But if it was Laurence Brown it all makes sense. He doesn't like violence, and he couldn't hit Josephine himself. With the booby trap he didn't have to see it happen.'

'Yes, I see,' I said slowly. 'It's just like putting the eserine in the insulin bottle.'

'Exactly.'

'Do you think Brenda knew?' I asked.

'I don't think she helped set the booby trap,' said Taverner, 'but I think the eserine was her idea, even if she made Laurence Brown do it himself. And with these letters, there's a clear case against both of them.'

He looked at me. 'So how does it feel to be marrying a very rich girl?' he asked.

I'd forgotten about the will. 'Sophia doesn't know yet,' I said. 'Do you want me to tell her?'

'Mr Gaitskill is going to tell everyone tomorrow, after the inquest,' said Taverner. 'I wonder what the family will say...'

Chapter 20

Nothing unusual happened at the inquest, because the police had said that they needed more time to collect the evidence.

We were all feeling more cheerful, however, because we'd heard from the hospital that Josephine was not as badly hurt as we thought, and she was getting better quickly. She wasn't allowed any visitors at the moment – not even her mother.

'Particularly not her mother,' murmured Sophia. 'I made that quite clear to Dr Gray. Mother would only <u>make a</u> big dramatic <u>scene</u>, which isn't good for someone who's been hit on the head.'

'You think of everything, don't you, darling,' I said. Aristide Leonides had been right to choose Sophia, I thought. She was already taking care of the family.

After the inquest, Mr Gaitskill came back to *Three Gables* and made his important announcement. He read Aristide Leonides' letter and then the will itself.

It was very interesting to watch. I was just sorry I couldn't watch everyone at the same time.

Philip's mouth was shut tightly, and he didn't speak. Magda, however, spoke as soon as Mr Gaitskill finished. 'Darling Sophia,' she said, 'how extraordinary – how romantic! But poor darling Roger. Now he doesn't have the money to save the company. Sophia, you *must* help Roger.'

'No,' said Clemency. 'We don't want anything!'

Roger stepped forward clumsily. 'We don't want any money,' he said, holding Sophia's hands. 'Clemency and I are going to Barbados to live a quiet life.' He smiled. 'But if I ever need anything, I'll ask the head of the family.'

'But Roger, you can't just go bankrupt and leave the country,' said Edith de Haviland. 'It makes the family, and Sophia, look bad – as if we didn't try to help you.'

Roger put his arms round his aunt and hugged her. 'Aunt Edith,' he said, 'you are a darling, but you don't understand what Clemency and I want!'

'None of you,' added Clemency, annoyed, 'understands Roger. You never have, and you never will! Come on, Roger.'

They left the room as Mr Gaitskill pretended to sort his papers. It was clear that he deeply disliked such family dramas.

When I looked at Sophia herself, she was standing up straight and her eyes were calm. She had just inherited an enormous fortune, but my first thought was that now she was alone, separate from the rest of her family. Her grandfather had believed that she was strong enough to be responsible for everyone else, but just then I felt very sorry for her.

'Congratulations, Sophia,' said Mr Gaitskill. 'You are a very rich woman. If you wish to discuss anything else, I'll be very happy to advise you.'

'What about Roger?' insisted Edith de Haviland.

'Roger,' said Mr Gaitskill quickly, 'must look after himself. He's a grown man. And he'll never be a successful businessman.' He looked at Sophia. 'If you save Associated Foods from bankruptcy, Roger is the wrong man to manage it.'

'I'm not going to save Associated Foods from bankruptcy,' said Sophia clearly. 'It would be a stupid thing to do.'

Mr Gaitskill looked at her and smiled to himself. Then he said goodbye and left the family alone together.

Everyone was silent for a moment, before Philip stood up. 'I must get back to the library,' he said. 'I have wasted a lot of time.'

'Father—' Sophia spoke cautiously. She stepped back as Philip looked at her coldly.

'I won't congratulate you,' he said. 'I am too shocked and <u>humiliated</u> that my father has ignored my lifelong <u>devotion</u> to him – yes – devotion!' For the first time his emotions broke through. 'How could he do this to me?' he exclaimed. 'He was always unfair to me – *always!*'

'Oh, Philip,' cried Edith de Haviland. 'Please don't think that!'

'He never cared for me,' said Philip, in a rough, low voice. 'It was always Roger. At least Father finally realized that Roger was a fool and a failure.' His handsome face was jealous. 'He didn't leave Roger anything either.'

'What about *me*?' said Eustace.

I saw that Eustace was shaking with violent emotion. His face was bright red and there were tears in his eyes. '*How* could Grandfather do this to me?' he said, his voice high and angry. 'I *hate* him. I'll never forgive him as long as I live. I wanted him to die. I wanted to get out of this house. Now Sophia is in charge and I wish I was dead…' He rushed out of the room.

'He has no self-control,' said Edith de Haviland quietly.

'I know just how Eustace feels,' said Magda. 'The poor darling! I must go after him.'

'Now, Magda—' Edith hurried after her.

Sophia stayed behind, looking at her father. But Philip again looked at her coldly, quite in control of himself once more.

'You've managed things very cleverly, Sophia,' he said and went out of the room.

'That was a cruel thing to say,' I said to Sophia, holding her in my arms. 'Your grandfather shouldn't have done this to you.'

'He thought I could bear it,' said Sophia, 'and I can. But I don't like Father and Eustace being so upset.'

'Your mother's all right.'

'But she won't like asking me for money for her new play,' said Sophia.

'What will you say if she does?' I asked curiously.

Sophia stood up very straight. 'I'll say no,' she said. 'It's a bad play and it will be a failure. It's a waste of money.'

I laughed. 'That's why your grandfather left everything to you,' I said. 'You're just like him.'

CHAPTER 21

I was sorry that Josephine had missed all the drama – she would have enjoyed it. She was getting better very quickly and would soon be home. But before she came back, one more important event took place.

I was in the garden one morning with Brenda – who said that she needed some exercise – and Sophia. After a while Brenda said abruptly, 'You're <u>giving</u> Laurence <u>the sack</u>, Sophia. Why?'

'We're making other arrangements for Eustace,' Sophia said quietly. 'And Josephine is going to Switzerland.'

'Well, you've upset Laurence very much. He feels you don't trust him.'

Sophia didn't answer and at that moment a car arrived in front of the house, and Chief Inspector Taverner stepped out. He went into the house.

'Why have the police come back?' said Brenda nervously. 'What do they want now?'

I thought I knew why they had come – because of the letters. Taverner came out of the house again and walked over to us. He spoke to Brenda in his official voice. 'Brenda Leonides, I am arresting you on suspicion of murdering Aristide Leonides with eserine on September 19th.'

Brenda completely lost control of herself. She held on to me and screamed, 'No, no, it isn't true! Charles, tell them! I didn't do it. I don't know anything about it. Don't let them take me away. *It isn't true*, I haven't done anything…'

It was a horrible scene. All I could do was try and calm her down. I told her that I would arrange for a lawyer for her – that a lawyer would help her with everything.

'Come along, Mrs Leonides,' said Taverner. 'We have to go now.'

'Laurence,' she said, staring at Taverner. 'What have you done to Laurence?'

'Mr Laurence Brown is also under arrest,' said Taverner.

At this news Brenda fell to the ground. The tears fell down her face as Taverner quietly helped her towards the car. Laurence Brown came out of the house with a police officer, and they all got into the car and drove away.

Sophia was pale and upset. 'It's horrible, Charles,' she said. 'You must get her a really good lawyer.' She sighed deeply. 'But why have they been arrested now?'

I explained that the police had found love letters from Brenda and Laurence. 'It *is* horrible, Sophia,' I added, 'but isn't it what we wanted? You said yourself it would be all right if the right person had killed your grandfather. Brenda was the right person, wasn't she? Brenda or Laurence?'

'Don't say that, Charles, you make me feel awful.'

'But it's true, isn't it? Now things can go back to normal – and we can get married. Your family are cleared of suspicion. Of course, none of you really had a motive.'

Sophia's face suddenly went white. 'Except me, Charles,' she said. 'I had a motive. I knew about the will.'

'What?' I stared at her. I suddenly felt cold.

'I knew that Grandfather had left his money to me. He told me. He said I must look after the family when he was gone.'

'Why didn't you tell me?'

'When there was such confusion with the will, I thought perhaps he'd made a mistake, or changed his mind. I didn't want him to leave everything to me – I was afraid.'

'Afraid?' I said. 'Why?'

'Because – because of the murder.'

So Sophia had been afraid that she would be suspected of murder. I understood now why she had refused to be engaged to me, and why she desperately wanted to know the truth.

As we walked back towards the house, I suddenly remembered something Sophia had said – that she supposed she *could* murder someone, but only for something really important.

CHAPTER 22

Before we reached the house, we met Roger and Clemency. 'Hello, you two,' said Roger. 'I see the police have arrested that horrible woman and her boyfriend at last. I hope they're both hanged[8].'

Clemency frowned. 'Don't be so cruel, Roger,' she said.

'Cruel?' said Roger 'Rubbish! They poisoned a helpless old man! I loved my father, don't you understand? I loved him.'

'I know, Roger, I know,' said Clemency.

We went towards the house. Roger and Sophia walked ahead and I walked behind with Clemency. 'The police should let us leave now,' she told me.

'Do you want to go so soon?' I asked.

'I'm desperate to go.' I looked at Clemency in surprise. 'Don't you understand, Charles?' she continued. 'I'm fighting for my happiness – and Roger's. I don't want Roger to stay here in England – I want him to come away with me. I want him all to myself, right away from his family.'

I hadn't realized how desperately Clemency loved Roger. I remembered what Edith de Haviland had said – that she loved her family, 'but not *too* much'. Had Edith been thinking of Clemency?

A car drove up to the front door and Josephine and Magda got out. Apart from the bandage round her head, Josephine looked very well. 'I want to look at the fish in the lake,' she said.

'Darling,' said Magda, 'come in and lie down for a while first. I'll get you some soup.'

'I don't want to lie down,' said Josephine. 'And I hate soup. I'm quite all right.'

Magda looked doubtful. I knew that Josephine had been kept safely in hospital until Brenda and Laurence had been arrested. 'I'll look after her,' I said to Magda, as Josephine went to see the fish.

When we got there, I asked Josephine if she wanted to hear about what had happened. 'Do you know that your grandfather left all his money to Sophia?'

'Mother told me,' Josephine said, sounding bored. 'Anyway, I knew already. I heard Grandfather tell Sophia.'

'Were you listening at the door again?'

'Yes. I like listening,' said Josephine. 'I heard what Grandfather said about me. Nannie doesn't like it when I listen.'

I changed the subject to something I thought would excite her. 'Chief Inspector Taverner has arrested Brenda and Laurence.'

'Yes, I know,' she said, still bored.

'How can you know? It's only just happened.'

'We passed their car on the road,' she said. 'Brenda and Laurence were inside, so of course I knew they'd been arrested.'

'I'm sorry,' I said, 'but I had to tell the police about the letters. I found them in the attic. You could have told them yourself if you hadn't been knocked out.'

Josephine touched her head carefully. 'I could have been killed,' she said, sounding pleased. 'I told you it was time for the second murder. It was stupid to hide those letters in the attic. I knew Laurence had hidden something there when I saw him coming out of the attic.'

'But I thought—' I stopped as we heard Edith de Haviland's voice, calling, 'Josephine, Josephine, come here at once.'

Josephine sighed. 'It's Aunt Edith, so I have to go.' She ran across the garden, and I followed more slowly. When Josephine had gone inside, I was left alone with Edith de Haviland. She looked very tired and old.

'I'm glad it's over,' she said to me. 'Do you think Brenda and Laurence will be found guilty?'

'I don't know,' I admitted. 'I don't know how much evidence the police have. There are love letters.'

Edith looked very grim. 'I'm not happy about this, Charles. I don't like Brenda in fact I dislike her very much. But I feel it's my responsibility to make sure she's treated fairly.'

'And Laurence?'

'Laurence is a man,' she said. 'He must look after himself. But Aristide would never forgive me if…' She didn't finish. Instead she suggested that we should go in for lunch, and I explained that I was driving back to London.

'Will you take me with you?' she asked. 'And not tell anyone?' I was surprised, but I did as she asked.

We didn't speak much on the journey. When I asked her where I should stop, she said, 'Harley Street.'

Harley Street was where all the best London doctors worked. I felt uneasy. 'I hope—' I began and stopped.

'That's why I didn't want to tell anyone,' Edith said. 'They'll just make a fuss.'

'I'm very sorry,' I said.

'Don't worry,' she said. 'I've had a very good life.' She smiled. 'And it's not finished yet.'

CHAPTER 23

After a quick visit to my father, who was busy, I went out for a drink with Chief Inspector Taverner. 'Well,' he said, 'the case is over at last.' But he didn't sound very happy about it.

'Do you think Brenda and Laurence will be found guilty?' I asked him.

'It's impossible to say,' he replied. 'There's no proof – and no definite or direct evidence against them. It's the same in a lot of murder cases.'

'What about the letters?'

'The letters say things like "it won't be long now" but they never mention poison. They could argue that all they meant was that Aristide Leonides was so old he was sure to die soon.'

'And what do *you* think – are they guilty?' I asked.

He looked at me with no expression on his face. 'I don't think anything, Charles. I've done my duty, and it's been decided to send them to trial.'

That's how I knew that Taverner wasn't satisfied.

A few days later I talked to my father about the case. Like Taverner, he said that there was enough evidence against Brenda and Laurence to send them to trial.

'That's not what I'm talking about,' I said. 'With your experience, do you think they're guilty?'

'To be honest with you, Charles, I just – don't know! They *could* be guilty, but I'm just not sure – and I wish I was.'

We were silent for a while, before my father said, 'So tell me, Charles, what do *you* think? Do you think that one of the Leonides family is the real murderer?'

'Yes, I do,' I finally admitted. 'Because that's what they think themselves.'

'Do they?' said my father. 'That's very interesting.'

'Only Roger is sure it's Brenda,' I continued. 'The others don't think so.'

'So who do you think it is?' my father asked quietly. 'Sophia?'

'No! Of course not, no!'

'But you're not completely sure, are you?' said my father. 'Even if you won't admit it. What about the others?'

'I can think of reasons – though not always good reasons – why they all could have killed Aristide Leonides,' I said. 'Philip has always been very jealous of Roger, and he could have poisoned his father to make sure that Roger's company went bankrupt. I don't think Magda is involved, and although she suddenly wants Josephine to go to school in Switzerland, I think it's because she's afraid that Josephine knows something. And she would never hit Josephine on the head.'

'Why not, Charles?' said my father. 'Don't you read the news? Mothers often dislike one or more of their children. Who else is there? What about Roger?'

'I'm sure that Roger didn't kill his father. But his wife might have done it.' I told him about my conversation with Clemency.

'And Edith,' I continued, 'Edith de Haviland might have done it, if she had a good reason. But I don't know why.'

'Would she hit the child on the head?'

'No,' I said slowly. 'I don't believe she would. Which reminds me – Josephine said something that doesn't fit in, but I can't quite remember what it was…'

'You'll remember soon,' said my father. 'Anyone else?'

'Well,' I said, 'it could be Eustace. He didn't like his grandfather and he has been behaving very strangely. And he's the only one who I think could knock out Josephine if she knew something about him – and she does seem to know everything. She writes it down in a little book—' I stopped.

'What's the matter?' asked my father.

'I've just remembered what Josephine said!' I exclaimed. 'We thought that Josephine's room was searched because of the letters. But Josephine told me that it was Laurence who hid the letters in the attic. She saw him and found the letters, but left them where they were.'

'Well?'

'That means that it wasn't the letters that someone was looking for in Josephine's room. It must have been something else – her little black book where she writes everything down. If Josephine still has that book—' I stood up.

'Then she still isn't safe,' said my father. 'Is that what you were going to say?'

'Yes,' I said. 'She won't be out of danger until she leaves for Switzerland.'

'I think you're right about the danger,' said my father. 'You should go to *Three Gables* at once.'

'Is it Eustace?' I asked him desperately. 'Clemency?'

'I think the facts point clearly in one direction,' my father said gently. 'I'm surprised you don't see it yourself. I think—'

At that moment a police officer knocked on the door. 'I know you asked not to be disturbed, sir, but Miss Leonides is on the telephone. She says it's urgent.'

I quickly picked up the telephone, and heard Sophia's voice say desperately, 'Charles, it isn't over. The murderer is still here.'

'What's wrong, Sophia? Is it – Josephine?'

'It's not Josephine,' said Sophia. 'It's Nannie. Josephine didn't drink her <u>cocoa</u>, and left it on a table. Nannie didn't want to waste it, so she drank it.'

'Poor Nannie. Is she very ill?'

'Oh, Charles,' said Sophia. 'She's *dead*.'

CHAPTER 24

It was like a terrible dream.

Taverner and I drove back quickly to Swinly Dean, just as we had before. On the journey I kept saying to myself that it hadn't been Brenda and Laurence. They had fallen in love with each other and written romantic letters, but they hadn't poisoned Aristide Leonides – or Nannie.

As we went through the front door I saw a big pile of luggage in the hall. Clemency came down the stairs. 'You're just in time to say goodbye, Charles,' she said. 'We're leaving tonight.'

'But surely you can't go now?' I said with surprise. 'Nannie is dead.'

'Nannie's death has nothing to do with us,' said Clemency. 'Roger and I were upstairs packing, and we didn't come down at all when Josephine's cocoa was on the hall table.'

'Can you prove that?' I said.

'Roger and I are going away,' said Clemency angrily. 'Why would we want to poison Nannie?'

'You might not have meant to poison Nannie.'

'We wouldn't poison Josephine, either.'

'But Josephine knows a lot about people,' I said. 'She—'

I stopped as Josephine herself appeared, eating an apple. Her eyes shone with excitement. 'Nannie's been poisoned,' she said. 'Just like Grandfather. It's very exciting, isn't it?'

'Aren't you upset about it?' I demanded. 'Didn't you like Nannie?'

'Not really. She was always telling me not to do things.'

'Do you like anybody, Josephine?' asked Clemency.

'I love Aunt Edith,' Josephine said. 'I love her very much. And I could love Eustace if he let me, but he's so horrible to me. I won't tell him what I've found out – that now I *know*.'

There was a moment's silence. Josephine stared at Clemency. I heard a noise from behind one of the doors, but when I opened it there was no one there.

I felt uneasy. As Edith de Haviland came down the stairs, I took hold of Josephine's arm and led her firmly into an empty room. I made her sit down in a chair while I sat opposite her. 'Now, Josephine,' I said, 'we're going to have a talk. What exactly do you know? Do you know who poisoned your cocoa?'

Josephine nodded.

'And you know who poisoned your grandfather?'

Josephine nodded again.

'And who knocked you on the head?'

Again Josephine nodded.

'Then you're going to tell me everything – now – and then we'll tell the police.'

'I won't,' said Josephine. 'I won't tell the police anything. They're stupid. They thought Brenda and Laurence did it. *I* didn't think so. So I made a test – and now I know I'm right.' She sounded very pleased with herself.

I tried hard to be patient. 'I know you're very clever, Josephine,' – she looked pleased – 'but don't you realize that you're in danger?'

'Of course I am,' said Josephine. 'In some books lots of people are killed.'

'This isn't a detective story – this is real life! You must tell me what you know.'

'You don't understand,' said Josephine. 'I might not *want* to tell. I might – be fond of the person.'

She paused. 'And if I *do* tell,' she continued, 'I'll do it properly, with everybody sitting together. I'll talk about all the clues, and then say suddenly, "It was *you*!"'

She pointed her finger just as Edith de Haviland entered the room.

'Josephine, throw that apple away,' said Edith, 'and wash your hands. I'm taking you out in the car.' She looked at me. 'It's safer out of the house. We'll go and get an ice cream.'

Josephine looked pleased. 'Can I have two?'

'Perhaps,' said Edith. 'Now go and get your coat, it's cold outside today. Charles, can you go with her? I must quickly write a few letters.'

She sat down at the desk, and I went upstairs with Josephine. Sophia came into the room, looking pale and nervous, as Josephine was getting ready. 'Charles,' she said with surprise. 'I didn't know you were here.'

'I'm going out with Aunt Edith,' said Josephine importantly. 'We're going to have ice creams.'

Sophia frowned as we went back downstairs to find Edith, who was just putting her two letters into envelopes. 'It's quite a nice day,' said Edith. 'Cold but clear.'

She was silent for a moment, looking down at the letters in her hand, and then she turned and kissed Sophia. 'Goodbye, dear,' Edith said. 'Don't worry too much. Some things just have to be accepted.'

She and Josephine got into the car and waved to us as they drove off.

'I suppose it's better to keep Josephine away for a while,' I said. 'But she must tell us what she knows.'

'She probably doesn't know anything,' Sophia said. 'She's just showing off and making herself look important.'

'I think it's more than that,' I said. 'Do they know yet what poison was in the cocoa?'

'They think it's Aunt Edith's heart medicine. There was a bottle full of pills, but now it's empty.'

'Isn't the medicine kept locked up?'

'Yes,' replied Sophia, 'but the key is quite easy to find.'

'But who was it?' I said. 'What do you think, Sophia?'

'I don't know,' she whispered. 'It's like a bad dream. Come outside with me, Charles. It's safer outside. I'm afraid to stay in this house.'

CHAPTER 25

We stayed outside in the garden for a long time. We didn't talk about the murders. Instead Sophia talked fondly about Nannie – the games they had played with her and the stories she had told them. I think this made Sophia feel better.

I wondered what Taverner was doing. More policemen had arrived, and Nannie's body had been taken away.

At last it was almost dark. 'We should go inside,' said Sophia with a shiver. 'Aunt Edith and Josephine haven't come back yet. Surely they should be back by now?'

I felt uneasy – what had happened to them?

We went inside and had tea with Magda. Philip stayed in the library. Magda didn't speak much, except to ask, 'Where are Edith and Josephine? They're out very late.'

I felt even more uneasy, so I went to speak to Taverner. 'The police will let us know if there's any news,' I told Sophia, who was alone in the room when I got back.

'I'm worried, Charles,' she said. 'Something must have happened.'

'It's not really late yet.'

'She kissed me goodbye…' said Sophia, with a strange expression on her face.

I didn't understand what she meant. We sat there for a while, pretending to read.

It was half past six when Taverner opened the door, and his serious face warned us that something was wrong. 'I'm sorry,' he said. 'I have bad news. We found Edith de Haviland's car at the bottom of the nearby stone <u>quarry</u>. Both people inside are dead – killed immediately.'

'Josephine!' Magda was standing at the door. Her voice rose as she cried, '*Josephine* – my baby!' Sophia put her arms round her mother.

'Wait a moment,' I said, as I remembered something. Edith de Haviland had not been carrying any letters when she got into the car. I ran out to the hall and found the letters on the table – half-hidden behind a vase.

The first letter was addressed to Chief Inspector Taverner, and I stood beside him as he read it.

When you read this letter I expect I will be dead. I wish to accept full responsibility for the deaths of Nannie and my brother-in-law, Aristide Leonides. I swear that Brenda Leonides and Laurence Brown are innocent. Dr Chavasse, of 783 Harley Street, will confirm that I have only a few more months to live. I prefer to end my life in this way and save two innocent people from being sent for trial for a murder they did not commit.

Edith de Haviland

Sophia, too, read the letter. '*Aunt Edith,*' she whispered. 'But why Josephine? Why did she take Josephine with her?'

Then – at last – I saw everything clearly. I realized that I was still holding Edith's second letter in my hand. It was addressed to me. I tore the envelope open and Josephine's little black notebook fell out. I opened it and saw the writing on the first page.

'We were wrong, Charles, weren't we?' Sophia whispered. 'Aunt Edith didn't do it.'

'No,' I said, 'she didn't.'

'It was – Josephine – wasn't it? It was Josephine.'

Together we looked down at the first page in the little black notebook.

'*Today I killed Grandfather.*'

CHAPTER 26

Afterwards I wondered how I could have been so <u>blind</u>. The truth was so obvious. Josephine, and only Josephine, was vain and <u>self-important</u>. She had loved to talk about the murder, and about how clever she was – and how stupid the police were.

Because she was a child, I had never thought that Josephine could be the murderer. But both murders could easily have been committed by a child. In fact her grandfather himself had told Josephine exactly what to do. And she read so many detective stories that she would know about fingerprints.

She had attacked herself, not really realizing that she could have been killed. There was a clue – the mud on the seat of the old chair. Josephine was the only person who would need to climb up on a chair to balance the heavy stone doorstop on the top of the door. Obviously it had missed her a few times – the marks in the floor showed that – but she had tried again, using her scarf so she didn't leave any fingerprints. Finally the doorstop had hit her.

We had all thought that Josephine was in danger, just as she wanted. She 'knew something' – she had been attacked!

I realized how she had carefully shown me – on purpose – where the attic was, so I found the letters. And she had made the mess in her room herself.

But when she came back from hospital, Josephine was unhappy. The case was over, Brenda and Laurence had been arrested and she herself wasn't getting much attention. So she stole Edith de Haviland's heart medicine, poisoned her own cocoa and left the cup on the hall table.

Did she know that Nannie would drink it? Possibly. Did Nannie, with a lifetime of experience with children, suspect Josephine?

And Edith – had she suspected too? Or had she known? I looked down at the letter in my hand.

Dear Charles

This letter is just for you, and for Sophia if you want to show it to her. I want someone to know the truth. I found Josephine's little notebook hidden in the garden. It confirms what I already suspected. I don't know if what I'm doing is right or wrong, but my life is nearly over, and I don't want Josephine to suffer for what she has done. If I am wrong, I hope I can be forgiven – I did it out of love. <u>Bless</u> you both.

Edith de Haviland

I gave the letter to Sophia, and when she had read it, we opened Josephine's little black notebook.

Today I killed Grandfather.

As we turned the pages, we saw Josephine's horribly childish motives for murder. Here are the important entries.

Grandfather wouldn't let me do ballet dancing so I made up my mind I would kill him. Then we should go to London to live and Mother wouldn't mind me doing ballet.

I don't want to go to Switzerland – I won't go. If Mother makes me I will kill her too – if I can get some poison.

Eustace made me very angry today. He says I am only a girl and that my detecting is silly. He wouldn't think I was silly if he knew it was me who did the murder.

I like Charles – but he is rather stupid. I have not decided yet who I shall say has done the murder. Perhaps Brenda and Laurence – Brenda is horrible to me, but I like Laurence.

Her last words were:

I hate Nannie, I hate her! She says I am only a little girl. She says I show off. She's making Mother send me away. I'm going to kill her, too – I think Aunt Edith's medicine will do it. If there is another murder, then the police will come back and it will all be exciting again.

Nannie's dead. I'm glad. I haven't decided yet where I'll hide the bottle with the pills. Perhaps in Aunt Clemency's room – or in Eustace's room. When I am dead I shall leave this notebook behind for the Chief of Police and they will see what a great criminal I was.

I closed the book. Sophia was crying. 'Oh, Charles – it's so awful. She's such a monster – but I also feel so much pity for her.'

I felt the same. I had liked Josephine, but she had been born with something wrong with her – she was the crooked child of the little *Crooked House*.

'What would have happened to her,' Sophia asked me, 'if she had lived?'

'I don't know,' I said. 'Perhaps she would have been sent to a special school – or a child's prison?'

'It's better this way,' Sophia said with a shiver. 'But I don't like Aunt Edith taking the blame.'

'It was her decision,' I said. 'I don't suppose anyone will find out. Brenda and Laurence will be free to go and there won't be a trial.

'And you, Sophia,' I added, holding her hands, 'will marry me. We'll go away together and you won't have to think about your family for a while. You can think about me instead.'

'Aren't you afraid to marry me, Charles?' said Sophia, looking straight into my eyes.

'Not at all,' I said. 'Why should I be? Poor little Josephine inherited all the worst from your families. But you, Sophia, have inherited the best. Your grandfather thought so and he, my darling, was always right.'

'I love you, Charles,' said Sophia. 'And I will marry you.' She looked down at the notebook. 'Poor Josephine.'

'Poor Josephine,' I said.

♦ ◆ ♦

'What really happened, Charles?' my father asked me.

I never lie to my father. 'It wasn't Edith de Haviland,' I told him. 'It was Josephine.'

My father nodded his head gently. 'Yes,' he said. 'I thought it was. Poor child…'

◆ Character list ◆

Charles Hayward: a young man who wants to marry Sophia Leonides. He tells the story

Sophia Leonides: the granddaughter of Aristide Leonides, and the eldest child of Philip and Magda

Aristide Leonides: a very rich – and old – businessman who is the father of Roger and Philip, and grandfather of Sophia, Eustace and Josephine

Mr Hayward: Charles' father, the Assistant Commissioner of Scotland Yard, London's police headquarters

Chief Inspector Taverner: the police officer in charge of the murder case

Edith de Haviland: the sister of the first Mrs Leonides, the aunt of Roger and Philip and the great-aunt of Sophia, Eustace and Josephine

Philip (Phil) Leonides: the second son of Aristide Leonides, who is married to Magda, and is the father of Sophia, Eustace and Josephine

Magda Leonides: an actress, who is married to Philip and is the mother of Sophia, Eustace and Josephine

Roger Leonides: the eldest son of Aristide Leonides, who is married to Clemency

Clemency Leonides: a scientist, who is married to Roger

Brenda Leonides: the second, much younger wife of Aristide Leonides

Laurence Brown: the young man who teaches Eustace and Josephine

Eustace Leonides: the son of Philip and Magda, and grandson of Aristide

Josephine Leonides: the second daughter of Philip and Magda, and granddaughter of Aristide

Mr Gaitskill: Aristide Leonides' lawyer

Nannie: the Leonides' family servant

◆ CULTURAL NOTES ◆

1. Nursery rhymes
Traditional nursery rhymes, like the one this story begins with, are said by almost every child in the UK when they are growing up. They are a kind of poem, and many of them are actually very old – sometimes hundreds of years old – but usually people have forgotten the original meaning. Children enjoy them because they are fun, simple and comforting. When you hear them again as an adult, however, sometimes you realize that some of them are very strange, perhaps even a little frightening. The story of Aristide Leonides and his family certainly makes you think about the 'crooked man' nursery rhyme in a different way.

2. World War II
The story begins during World War II (1939–1945) in Cairo. The 'Allies' (which included the UK, the Soviet Union, the USA, and China) were fighting the 'Axis powers' (which included Germany, Italy, and Japan) for control of North Africa. Sophia and Charles are working for the British Government in Egypt when they meet.

During the war, many people had to leave home to fight or work, like Charles and Sophia. It was a time when people could make new and unexpected friendships or fall in love. However, they then often had to move to other places and could not contact their friends for months or years. This is why Charles did not want to make marriage plans at the beginning of the story.

Many large cities in the UK, especially London, were attacked by aeroplanes and bombs. These attacks destroyed a lot of buildings and killed many people across the country. Philip Leonides' family went to live with Aristide Leonides because he had a large house, and it was outside of London in the suburbs, so there was less danger from bombs.

3. Telegrams
In the 1940s, the quickest way to send an urgent message was by telegram. Because the sender had to pay for each word, people only wrote the most important words, which makes the style of telegrams very different from ordinary English.

4. Deaths column in newspapers
Daily newspapers were very important in the UK. People often read a *national* newspaper in the morning at breakfast, and then a *local* newspaper in the evening. Besides official news, there were many other short sections, called 'columns': for society and entertainment news, for selling and buying things, etc. When a new baby was born, a couple got married, or a person died, their family announced the news in the Births, Marriages, or Deaths columns.

5. Scotland Yard and the police
Scotland Yard is the headquarters – the main building – of the Greater London Police. Small, local crimes in and around London are the responsibility of local police stations (where Chief Inspector Taverner works), but in difficult or important cases, police officers from Scotland Yard with more experience and more power (like Charles' father) help the local police. Scotland Yard is very famous in UK detective stories. The headquarters is still in London, but has now moved to a new site and is called '*New* Scotland Yard'.

6. Diabetes and injections
An important part of the story is that Aristide Leonides needs to have injections of insulin. This is because he has diabetes, which means that his body cannot control the amount of sugar in his blood. If there is too much sugar, it damages the body, and can even kill. Insulin can control how much sugar there is, but you must inject it directly into the blood,

and you must do it regularly – many people have to inject themselves once a day or more.

7. Aristide Leonides' house

Aristide Leonides was a successful businessman with enough money to design and build his own house. When Aristide built his house, he wanted it to look like a traditional little English house. Unfortunately, he built a very large house so although it had traditional English features, it looked very strange to English eyes.

8. Inquests

When the police investigate a sudden, violent or suspicious death (such as Aristide Leonides' unexpected death), they often hold a public investigation called an inquest to find out why the person died.

At the inquest, a group of people hears medical evidence, as well as evidence from any other people that may be useful. The family of the person who died and members of the public can also go to the inquest to watch.

If the inquest shows that the death was actually a murder, then the police can investigate, arrest and question any suspects. If the police decide that there is enough evidence against a suspect, then this person is officially sent for trial in a court to decide if they are guilty or innocent.

At the time of this story, when a trial proved that someone was guilty of murder, this person could be punished by hanging. A rope was tied round the person's neck, and the support was taken away from under their feet, killing the person. The last hanging for murder in the UK took place in 1964, and this punishment was officially stopped later.

9. Inheritance

When the story was written, if a man died without a will, all his money and property would usually go to his wife. If someone wanted to change this, and control what *other* people inherited, they had to write a will. This document must be signed by two people who have no connection with the money or property in the will – in this story, Aristide Leonides asks two of the servants in the house to sign the will to make it legal.

Because the law can be complicated and difficult, people often use a lawyer to help them write a will, but even if the will is not checked by a lawyer, it is still legal as long as two witnesses have signed it.

10. Bankruptcy

If a company has a lot of problems and finally does not have enough money to pay its debts, it needs to use the 'bankruptcy laws' to protect itself and the people it needs to pay.

Bankruptcy laws control how much money a company must pay, and who should receive the money. In many countries now, people consider that bankruptcy is a normal part of the economy, though it has serious consequences for the people involved. When this story was written, however, bankruptcy was still a terrible scandal or shame, not only for the person who was bankrupt, but also for their whole family.

✦ Glossary ✦

abrupt ADJECTIVE
Someone who is **abrupt** speaks in a rather rude, unfriendly way.

airy ADJECTIVE
If a building or room is **airy**, it has a lot of fresh air inside, usually because it is large.

alibi COUNTABLE NOUN
If you have an **alibi**, you can prove that you were somewhere else when a crime was committed.

assistant commissioner
COUNTABLE NOUN
The **Assistant Commissioner** is the third most senior police officer in London.

attic COUNTABLE NOUN
An **attic** is a room at the top of a house just below the roof.

bankrupt ADJECTIVE
People or organizations that go **bankrupt** do not have enough money to pay their debts.

bindweed UNCOUNTABLE NOUN
Bindweed is a wild plant that winds itself around other plants and makes it difficult for them to grow.

bless PHRASE
Bless is used in expressions such as 'bless you' or 'God bless' to express affection, thanks, or good wishes.

blind ADJECTIVE
If you say that someone is **blind** to a fact or a situation, you mean that they ignore it or are unaware of it, although you think that they should take notice of it or be aware of it.

booby trap COUNTABLE NOUN
A **booby trap** is something such as a bomb which is hidden or disguised and which causes death or injury when it is touched.

burst open PHRASAL VERB
When a door **bursts open**, it opens very suddenly and violently because someone pushes it or there is great pressure behind it.

case COUNTABLE NOUN
A **case** is a crime or mystery that the police are investigating.

clumsily ADVERB
If you do something **clumsily**, you do it in a careless, awkward way, often so that things are knocked over or broken.

cocoa UNCOUNTABLE NOUN
Cocoa is a chocolate-flavoured hot drink usually made with milk.

concussion UNCOUNTABLE NOUN
If you suffer **concussion** after a blow to your head, you lose consciousness or feel sick or confused.

crooked ADJECTIVE
If you describe something as **crooked**, especially something that is usually straight, you mean that it is bent or twisted.

ADJECTIVE
If you describe a person or an activity as **crooked**, you mean that they are dishonest or criminal.

death certificate COUNTABLE NOUN
A **death certificate** is an official certificate signed by a doctor which states the cause of a person's death.

detect VERB
To **detect** means to find or discover things by making an investigation.

devotion UNCOUNTABLE NOUN
Devotion is great love, affection, or admiration for someone.

diabetes UNCOUNTABLE NOUN
Diabetes is a medical condition in which someone cannot control the amount of sugar in their blood.

dignity UNCOUNTABLE NOUN
If someone does something with **dignity**, they do it in a calm, controlled, and admirable way.

doorstop COUNTABLE NOUN
A **doorstop** is a heavy object that you use to keep a door open.

drawing room COUNTABLE NOUN
A **drawing room** is a room, especially a large room in a large house, where people sit and relax, or entertain guests.

dressing-gown COUNTABLE NOUN
A **dressing-gown** is a long, loose garment which you wear over your night clothes or underwear when you are not in bed.

eldest ADJECTIVE
The **eldest** person in a group or family is the one who was born before all the others.

embezzle TRANSITIVE VERB
If someone **embezzles** money that has been put in their care, they take and use it illegally for their own purposes.

erase TRANSITIVE VERB
If you **erase** something such as writing or a mark, you remove it, usually by rubbing it with something.

eserine UNCOUNTABLE NOUN
Eserine is a very poisonous substance that is used in some medicines but that can kill people.

exclaim TRANSITIVE VERB
If someone **exclaims** something, they say it suddenly, loudly, or emphatically, often because they are excited, shocked, or angry.

exit line COUNTABLE NOUN
An **exit line** is something someone says as they leave a room or stage.

eyedrops PLURAL NOUN
Eyedrops are a kind of medicine that you put in your eyes one drop at a time.

fairy story COUNTABLE NOUN
A **fairy story** is a story for children involving magical events and imaginary creatures. You can say that something is 'like a fairy story' if it is so wonderful you can hardly believe it is real.

fingerprint COUNTABLE NOUN
Fingerprints are marks made by a person's fingers which show the lines on the skin. Everyone's fingerprints are different, so they can be used to identify criminals.

firmly ADVERB
If you do or say something **firmly**, you do or say it in a very determined way.

frown COUNTABLE NOUN
A **frown** is an expression in which someone's eyebrows become drawn together, because they are annoyed, worried, or puzzled, or because they are thinking.

gable COUNTABLE NOUN
A **gable** is the triangular part at the top of the end wall of a building, between the two sloping sides of the roof.

give (someone) the sack PHRASE
If your employer **gives** you **the sack**, they tell you that you can no longer work for them because you have done something that they did not like or because your work was not good enough.

great-aunt COUNTABLE NOUN
Your **great-aunt** is the aunt of one of your parents.

grimly ADVERB
If you do or say something **grimly**, you do or say it in a very serious way, usually because something sad or bad has happened.

grind TRANSITIVE VERB
If you **grind** something under your foot, you press and rub it hard into the ground using small circular or sideways movements of your foot.

helpless ADJECTIVE
If you are **helpless**, you do not have the strength or power to do anything to control a situation or protect yourself.

humiliated ADJECTIVE
If you feel **humiliated**, you feel
ashamed and stupid because of
something someone has done
to you.

hush PHRASE
You say '**Hush!**' to someone in
who is upset, crying, or shouting,
to ask or encourage them to be
quiet.

inherit TRANSITIVE VERB
If you **inherit** money or property,
you receive it from someone who
has died.

injection COUNTABLE NOUN
If you have an **injection**, a doctor
or nurse puts a medicine into
your body using a device with a
needle called a syringe.

inquest COUNTABLE NOUN
When an **inquest** is held, a public
official hears evidence about
someone's death in order to find
out the cause.

insulin UNCOUNTABLE NOUN
Insulin is a substance that
controls the level of sugar in
the blood, which most people
produce naturally in their body
but which people with diabetes
do not produce enough of.

ironically ADVERB
If you say something **ironically**,
you do not mean it and are
saying it as a joke.

judgement UNCOUNTABLE NOUN
Judgement is the ability to make
sensible guesses about a
situation or sensible decisions
about what to do.

knitting UNCOUNTABLE NOUN
Knitting is the activity of making
something, such as an article of
clothing, from wool using large
needles. Someone's **knitting** is
something that they are making
from wool in this way.

knock out PHRASAL VERB
To **knock** someone out means to
cause them to become
unconscious.

lifeless ADJECTIVE
If you describe someone or something as **lifeless**, you mean they lack any lively or exciting qualities.

lifelong ADJECTIVE
Lifelong means existing or happening for the whole of a person's life.

-like SUFFIX
-like is used after a noun to make an adjective that describes something as similar to or typical of the noun. For example 'business-like' means 'in an efficient or unemotional way, as you would do in business'.

luxurious ADJECTIVE
If you describe something as **luxurious**, you mean that it is very comfortable and expensive.

make a scene PHRASE
If you **make a scene**, you embarrass people by publicly showing how angry or upset you are about something.

murmur TRANSITIVE VERB
If you **murmur** something, you say it very quietly, so that not many people can hear what you are saying.

my goodness PHRASE
People sometimes say '**my goodness**' to express surprise.

nursery rhyme COUNTABLE NOUN
A **nursery rhyme** is a poem or song for young children, especially one that is old or well known.

overhear TRANSITIVE VERB
If you **overhear** someone, you hear what they are saying when they are not talking to you and they do not know that you are listening.

play tricks with PHRASE
If someone **plays tricks with** something, they do something clever in order to deceive people.

poisoner COUNTABLE NOUN
A **poisoner** is someone who has deliberately killed or harmed another person using poison.

quarry COUNTABLE NOUN
A **quarry** is an area that is dug out from a piece of land or the side of a mountain in order to get stone or minerals.

ruthless ADJECTIVE
If you say that someone is **ruthless**, you mean that they will do anything necessary to achieve what they want, even if this involves being harsh or cruel.

Scotland Yard PROPER NOUN
Scotland Yard is the headquarters of the London police force, and is often used to refer to the police force or its detectives.

self-important ADJECTIVE
If you say that someone is **self-important**, you disapprove of them because they behave as if they are more important than they really are.

shrug your shoulders PHRASE
If you **shrug your shoulders**, you raise them to show that you are not interested in something or that you do not know or care about something.

sixpence COUNTABLE NOUN
A **sixpence** is an old British coin worth six old pence.

slyly ADVERB
If someone does something **slyly**, they do it in a way that keeps their feelings or intentions hidden in order to deceive someone.

snap VERB
If something **snaps** or if you **snap** it, it breaks suddenly, usually with a sharp cracking noise.

sneak INTRANSITIVE VERB
If you **sneak** somewhere, you move around quietly and secretly, trying not to be noticed.

soppy ADJECTIVE
If you describe someone or something as **soppy**, you mean that they are foolishly sentimental.

spy on PHRASAL VERB
If you **spy on** someone, you watch them secretly.

stiffly ADVERB
If you move **stiffly**, you move in a way that is formal and not relaxed, without bending your body.

stile COUNTABLE NOUN
A **stile** is an entrance to a field or path consisting of a step on either side of a fence or wall to help people climb over it.

strangle TRANSITIVE VERB
To **strangle** someone means to kill them by squeezing their throat tightly so that they cannot breathe.

suspect COUNTABLE NOUN
A **suspect** is a person who the police or authorities think may be guilty of a crime.

suspicion UNCOUNTABLE NOUN
Suspicion is a belief or feeling that someone has committed a crime or done something wrong.

swear TRANSITIVE VERB
If you say that you **swear** something is true, you are saying very firmly that it is true.

syringe COUNTABLE NOUN
A **syringe** is a small tube with a thin hollow needle at the end. Syringes are used, for example, for injecting drugs or for taking blood from someone's body.

tangle TRANSITIVE VERB
If something gets **tangled up** or **tangled** with something else, they become twisted together so that they are caught or trapped.

telegram COUNTABLE NOUN
A **telegram** was a message that was sent by telegraph and then printed and delivered to someone's home or office.

timber COUNTABLE NOUN
The **timbers** of a house are the large pieces of wood that have been used to build it.

twig COUNTABLE NOUN
A **twig** is a very small thin branch that grows out from a main branch of a tree or bush.

twist INTRANSITIVE VERB
If part of your body **twists**, it moves into an unusual, uncomfortable, or bent position.

twitch INTRANSITIVE VERB
If part of your body **twitches**, it makes a little jumping movement.

unreal ADJECTIVE
If you say that a situation is **unreal**, you mean that it is so strange that you find it difficult to believe it is happening.

vain ADJECTIVE
If you describe someone as **vain**, you disapprove of them because they are very proud of their own appearance, intelligence, or abilities.

viciously ADVERB
If you do something **viciously**, you do it in a very violent or cruel way.

wash-house COUNTABLE NOUN
A **wash-house** is a small building outside a house where clothes were washed in the past.

weed COUNTABLE NOUN
A **weed** is a wild plant that grows in gardens or fields of crops and prevents the plants that you want from growing properly.

wicked ADJECTIVE
You use **wicked** to describe someone or something that is very bad and that aims to harm people.

will COUNTABLE NOUN
A **will** is a document in which you declare what you want to happen to your money and property when you die.

witness COUNTABLE NOUN
A **witness** is someone who writes their name on a document that you have signed, to confirm that it really is your signature.

yard COUNTABLE NOUN
A **yard** is a flat outside area with a stone, brick or concrete floor and often with a wall around it.

COLLINS ENGLISH READERS ONLINE

Go online to discover the following useful resources for teachers and students:

- Downloadable audio of the story

- Classroom activities, including a plot synopsis

- Student activities, suitable for class use or for self-studying learners

- A level checker to ensure you are reading at the correct level

- Information on the Collins COBUILD Grading Scheme

All this and more at **www.collinselt.com/readers**

COLLINS ENGLISH READERS

Do you want to read more at your reading level?
Try these:

AGATHA CHRISTIE MYSTERIES

Sparkling Cyanide 978-0-00-826234-1
They Do It With Mirrors 978-0-00-826236-5
A Pocket Full of Rye 978-0-00-826237-2
Destination Unknown 978-0-00-826238-9
4.50 From Paddington 978-0-00-826239-6
Cat Among the Pigeons 978-0-00-826240-2
Appointment with Death 978-0-00-826233-4
Peril at End House 978-0-00-826232-7
The Murder at the Vicarage 978-0-00-826231-0

Find out more at **www.collinselt.com/readers**